The Burlwood Forest Trilogy

BURLWOOD FOREST

o

THROUGH THE WOODS

o

MANY FIELDS

The Burlwood Forest Trilogy

MANY FIELDS

Written and Illustrated by

JOHN CHOQUETTE

· pumpernickel art ·

Printed in the United States of America
First Printing, 2016
ISBN 978-0-692-79005-2

Pumpernickel Art
Raleigh, NC
www.burlwoodforest.com
@burlwoodforest

For my amazing wife, Anna. You are the best!

John Choquette

Michael Pumpernickel had never been bored before. Seriously, it was his first time!

"In my 13 years of existence, I've never felt like this. It's weird," Michael thought.

I know what you're thinking. Wait a second...HOLD THE PHONE! Michael's not 13, he's 11! Okay, you're right. Well, you WERE right. NOW he's 13. Two years have passed in Some Town, and Michael has spent almost all of it in one place...his room.

That's not so bad, right? He LOVES his room! But somewhere is never quite as fun if you're being held against your will. Michael was definitely being held against his will! His parents had hired a nanny to keep an eye on him.

So, it wasn't really all that great of a situation. No big deal though, it could have been worse. Well, it actually WAS worse. His nanny was one of the Harrington twins!

You know, one of Dapply's thugs? A henchman's henchman.

But Michael's parents did what they thought they had to do. I mean, Michael had missed almost a whole month of school! That was COMPLETELY out of character. They didn't want him on the 'streets.' Instead, they kept him inside where he could only LOOK at the 'streets.' Now, he would be safe!

At first, a bodyguard nanny seemed kind of extreme. In fact, the Pumpernickels had debated it for hours. But then they tasted the Twin's fettuccini and suddenly all bets were off. He was staying, possibly forever. I guess they didn't know he was an associate of an associate of a crazy, psycho killer fox. How could they?

Well, besides the fact that Michael kept telling them. Hey, that's a minor detail. The Twin was available. He had good rates. It was too good to be true!

He cooked dinner and did the dishes. He rescued stray cats and helped old ladies. He even taught one of the neighbor's kids to ride her bike! The Twin was a model citizen, an upstanding employee and the third, slightly older son they'd never had. He was perfect!

But the Pumpernickels must not have seen the way he looked at Michael when their backs were turned. Or the huge knife he kept under the table during dinner. No, to them, the Harrington Twin was a real dandy. Whatever that means.

You didn't expect Michael to behave though, did you? He HATED being locked up! Naturally, he tried to escape. From your typical bed sheet rope, to breaking his own leg (which actually happened when he fell out the window), his plans didn't work. Like, at all. The Harrington Twin was one step ahead of him every time.

Michael was stuck and no one came to save him. Not Crispin. Not his Grandpa. Well, especially, not his Grandpa. His parents would NEVER allow that!

In the weeks after Michael was taken from prison, Henry Pumpernickel was tried and convicted of disorderly conduct and aggravated assault in connection to the Some Town Fashion Week Riots. While he was in jail, the police 'coincidently' decided to revisit an unsolved case he just happened to have a connection to-

...a quadruple homicide during the founding of Burlwood Forest Village.

Maybe it was just convenience, but they decided after all of these years, Henry Pumpernickel was the murderer. Now he's on death row and is set to be executed in exactly one week.

Which, you know, isn't good.

But Michael wasn't worried about that. His Grandpa could always come back as a ghost. The REAL problem was that nothing else was wrong! With the Nervous Sleeve out of the way, Lord Piper had a clear path to world domination. What was stopping him?

The overall health of Some Town had never been better. The population was booming. Jobs were being created every day. In one of the most surprising modern day success stories, Jerry Mudwater had even led an initiative to build a massive shopping mall in the center of Burlwood Forest. That led to increased tourism and a new stadium for the Some Town Fright.

Yes, things were great and that was the problem. Michael had to figure out what was wrong before it was too late!

"Hey, Michael!" Mr. Pumpernickel said, his voice muffled through the door. "You've got to come down and see this! The Nature Channel is having a 'Vampires Destroying Big Things in a Big Way' marathon! If you hurry, maybe your mother will let me watch it!"

That's on the Nature Channel? Michael frowned.

"Are you alive in there?!?" Mr. Pumpernickel said, beating on the door. "This is a chance of a lifetime! Your mother always finds a way to interrupt my show and she's not here right now. We can watch it together!"

Michael gazed uneasily at the door as the Harrington Twin sneered at him from a chair in the corner of the room. The Twin took out his knife, sharpening it on the side of Michael's bed. It made a hideous screeching sound as it scraped against the metal.

"Hurry!" Mr. Pumpernickel said frantically.

Suddenly, the door opened and the scratching stopped. *YES!* Michael thought, grinning. *Dad HAD to have seen the Twin's knife! Now he'll have to believe me. This is even better than the time I invented sliced bread! Oh wait, that wasn't me...*

"Michael, why are you smiling like that? It's scaring Mr. Harrington," Mr. Pumpernickel said sternly.

Michael turned and saw the Twin sitting calmly in his chair. He had a triumphant expression on his face and the knife was nowhere to be seen.

Wait, really?!?!? What the devil...

"Now, I know that you're not happy with this arrangement, Michael, but it's the best we can do," Mr. Pumpernickel said, coming into the room and sitting down on Michael's bed. He had a fatherly look on his face, but he was unsure of what to do with his hands. Sighing, he awkwardly placed them on Michael's back.

The bed leg closest to the Twin snapped and they toppled to the floor.

"HOLY CROW!!!!!!" Mr. Pumpernickel yelled, grasping his knee. "What did you do?!?"

Michael shot an angry glance at the Twin, but he was already out of his chair and making his way toward them.

"I'm sorry, sir," the Twin said in a sympathetic tone. "I have no idea what he did. I can assure you I would NEVER have allowed that on my watch." He smiled and held out his hand to help Mr. Pumpernickel up.

"Of course, of course," Mr. Pumpernickel said, taking the Twin's hand and brushing off his shirt (his FAVORITE shirt, no less). "You've done a wonderful job for us Mr...ummm...You know," he laughed. "You never told us your first name!"

"That's quite alright, sir," the Twin said, offering Mr. Pumpernickel his chair. "You may call me whatever you like."

Just then, they heard the front door open.

"Your mother! Blast it all!" Mr. Pumpernickel said, rushing to the door. He gave Michael an angry look. "What about my show?!?"

"Oh, dear?" Mrs. Pumpernickel said, stopping him in his tracks. "Why don't you and Michael come down here and watch the news with me? There's just so many exciting things going on around town these days."

Mr. Pumpernickel turned around slowly, clenching his fists as he collapsed against the door. He seemed like he wanted to say something, but stopped himself, which was probably good because 'you'll pay for this' isn't very fatherly. Instead, he sighed.

"Coming, honey! Come on, Michael," he said, hanging his head. Michael thought he heard him whimper as he walked down the stairs.

I hate the news, Michael thought. *It's too realistic.* He stood up, glad to at least leave his room. He was surprised to see that the Twin wasn't following him. That was definitely not normal. Not bad, but not normal.

"Well, aren't you coming?" Michael snapped.

No, apparently not. The Twin was sprawled out on the ground with a vacant expression on his face. A pool of blood was forming below him.

Michael gasped and walked over for a better look. A knife, the SAME knife the Twin had sharpened on the bed, was sticking out his back. In his rush to put it away, he must have stabbed himself. And, you know, somehow not noticed for a brief period of time. Somehow...

"Egad! I've never had a murder occur in my bedroom before," Michael said, shocked. "At least not in real life, just in Distant Galaxy. What do I do?" He backed away from the body.

"MICHAEL!!!!" Mr. Pumpernickel yelled from the living room. "If I have to watch this you do too! Get down here this instant!"

Should I tell them?!?!? Michael wondered. *I don't want them to think I did that. That's a world of trouble!*

He decided it was probably best to tell them. After all, the blood was beginning to stain his carpet and he only had one floor in his room. He didn't want to have to fly everywhere. He didn't know how to fly!

But like...what should I do with him? he wondered, scratching his head. *This is entirely atypical.*

After thinking for a moment, Michael decided to do what any sensible person would do (and I truly hope that you never find yourself in this situation). He was going to roll the body down the stairs! Carefully, putting on his

Sneaky Pete and the Cool Brigade SneakGloves, he started to roll the Twin toward the door. Michael smiled, chuckling to himself.

"This isn't as bad as I thought," he said.

(You know, besides the whole dead guy thing...)

Suddenly, Michael banged his knee against the doorframe. "DERN FERN!!!!" he yelled, looking down to see what the problem was. Apparently the Twin had hit HIS knee on the other side of the door. Michael was going to have to turn him somehow to get him through.

"What's going on up there, Michael?" Mrs. Pumpernickel asked. "Your father and I miss you down here. They just did a story on wombats!"

Ever since Michael had come home from prison, his mother had tried to be nicer to him. She felt bad, thinking maybe she was the reason he'd snapped. Wait until she saw the body. Or, really, until he watched the news. HE might snap at that point.

"Nothing, Mom!" Michael said, in a tone that would have given him away if his parents hadn't been so distracted.

"Please hurry!" Mr. Pumpernickel said urgently. "I can't take much more of this!"

Michael's gloves were covered in blood. He grimaced, thinking about how much they had cost. *Fifteen box tops from Mr. Sugar's Choco Squares*!

"I may as well not delay the inevitable," he said, twisting the Twin's body and pushing him down the stairs.

THUMP! It was a long staircase.

Michael's mom screamed.

Maybe this wasn't such a good idea? he thought. There was blood everywhere, even on the walls. Michael paused halfway down the stairs. "If I take off my gloves, maybe they won't blame me? Good thinking, me," he said, throwing them down the hall into Ralph's room.

"What's up, Mom and Dad?" he said, casually walking into the room. Michael looked down at his hands, brushing some of the blood onto the drapes.

"Son, what's going on?" Mr. Pumpernickel asked, pointing to the Twin. He didn't look overly concerned to be missing the news. Mrs. Pumpernickel on the other hand, just stared, clutching her heart.

"Oh my goodness!" Michael said, faking surprise and rushing over. "What happened?!?!"

"We were hoping you could tell us," Mr. Pumpernickel said sternly.

"I don't know," Michael shrugged. "Maybe he fell down the stairs? Is he dead?"

"We wondered that too," Mr. Pumpernickel said, putting his ear to the Twin's chest. "No heartbeat. There sure is a lot of blood..."

"Blood. Blood. Blood," Mrs. Pumpernickel mumbled, her eyes wide.

"I'm afraid we don't understand you dear," Mr. Pumpernickel said. "You'll have to speak more clearly."

"Blood. Blood. So much blood."

"You'd think for someone who watches the news, she wouldn't be shocked," Michael laughed.

Mr. Pumpernickel glared at him. "This isn't funny, Michael. We have to figure out what to do. Hey, wait a second...is that a knife sticking out of his back?"

"What?!?!" Michael said, pretending to be flabbergasted. "No, no, of course not." He quickly pulled the knife out and put it in his pocket.

"Now, hold on," Mr. Pumpernickel said, holding his head. "Please tell me you didn't..."

"No way!" Michael said. "Dad, he tried to kill me!"

"So you killed him back?!?!?" Mr. Pumpernickel shouted. Michael had never heard his Dad raise his voice like this before. It was kind of scary.

"No, Dad, no," Michael frowned. "He's been trying to kill me for weeks! He accidently stabbed himself when he was putting his knife away earlier. You know, when you came into the room and stuff."

"Blood. Blood. Blood."

"But that doesn't make sense," Mr. Pumpernickel said, exasperated. "He was fine when I went in there."

"Apparently, not," Michael said, shrugging.

Mr. Pumpernickel sighed. "When your mother snaps out of it, she's not going to be very happy about this. What should we tell her?"

"Blood. Blood. Blood."

"Umm...that he quit?" Michael asked, hopefully.

Mrs. Pumpernickel blinked and looked down at the body. "MICHAEL SOCRATES, COME HERE THIS INSTANT!!!!" she yelled, turning red in the face.

"I'm right here, Mom," Michael said, starting to back away.

"Oh, well then," she said, smiling. "WELL THEN! Michael, what happened to Mr. Harrington? He was going to make us fettuccini tonight!"

"He fell down the stairs, Mom. And he got stabbed. Not in that order."

"My DRAPES!" Mrs. Pumpernickel said, tearing a large chunk out of her hair. "They're ruined! It's all ruined!"

"Dear, I think we can fix it," Mr. Pumpernickel said, nodding at Michael. "Your son has explained to me exactly what happened and..."

"MY SON?!?!?! What do you mean MY son?!?!?!"

"That's not what I meant, I..." Mr. Pumpernickel said, looking to Michael for help.

"I'll clean it up," Michael said, shrugging, hoping it would get him off the hook. He was just relieved the Twin wouldn't be following him around anymore. He was FREE!

"Of course you will," Mrs. Pumpernickel said, making a list in her head. "And we'll have to find a new nanny. No WAY we'll be letting you free after THIS stunt."

"But..."

"No buts, Michael," Mrs. Pumpernickel said sternly.

"Yeah!" Mr. Pumpernickel said, shaking his fist.

"Not helping, dear."

"Message received," he said, sitting on the ground before standing up and sitting in a chair.

"Let's just all take a deep breath," Mrs. Pumpernickel said, gritting her teeth. "Michael, come have a seat with us."

"Yes, come have a seat," Mr. Pumpernickel echoed.

"We can finish the news and then worry about this."

"Listen to your mother, Michael. We can...CONFOUND IT!" Mr. Pumpernickel snapped. He hated the news.

Michael stepped cautiously over the body and sat down next to his mother.

"Now, isn't this nice?" Mrs. Pumpernickel asked.

But they're talking about a rabid armadillo outbreak! Michael thought. Still, he was happy that the focus was off him, at least for a moment. He was safe now.

"Look who's on the news, dear!" Mrs. Pumpernickel said excitedly, turning to her husband. "You can't possibly want to turn it off now. He's your favorite!"

Mr. Pumpernickel glanced at the screen and smiled. "Ah, I guess you're right! You always are. But then again, who wouldn't like him? He's a hero!"

Michael looked up to see who they were talking about and a huge pit formed in his stomach.

It was Jerry Mudwater!

"Dad, you can't possibly like this guy!" Michael said angrily. "He's a complete..."

"MICHAEL!" Mrs. Pumpernickel said sternly.

"What?" Michael asked, confused.

"You were about to say something terrible!"

"No, I wasn't," Michael said.

"Yes, you were. You said, and I quote, 'Dad, you can't possibly like this guy! He's a complete...'"

"But you have no idea what I was going to say AFTER that," Michael frowned.

"GUYS, I'M WATCHING THE NEWS!" Mr. Pumpernickel shouted, turning up the volume.

"Yes, dear, we know that," Mrs. Pumpernickel said matter-of-factly, "but Michael..."

"Dad, you don't even like the news," Michael scoffed, shaking his head.

"You're right, but I like Jerry," Mr. Pumpernickel said, scooting to the edge of his seat.

"Wait a second," Mrs. Pumpernickel said, grabbing the remote and turning the sound off. She turned to her husband, her face red with anger. "YOU DON'T LIKE THE NEWS?!? WHY DON'T YOU LIKE THE NEWS?!? IS IT BECAUSE I LIKE THE NEWS? WELL, IS IT?!?"

*Oh, sandwiches...*Michael though, rolling his eyes.

"No, I, it's just..."

"You better think LONG and HARD about your answer if you don't want to sleep on the couch tonight!"

"But I just..." Mr. Pumpernickel sighed and slid back into his seat.

"Now, look. We've missed his whole speech," Mrs. Pumpernickel said angrily.

Michael looked up and saw Jerry shaking hands with the crowd, smiling and laughing as he made his way to a stretch limousine parked by the curb. A campaign button that said, 'Jerry Mudwater for Mayor,' was affixed to his jacket. He was closely followed by a group of menacing looking rhinos with dark sunglasses.

How in the world does nobody notice that those aren't people? Michael thought. *Is that not weird?*

"Look, dear!" Mrs. Pumpernickel said excitedly. "Jerry's running for mayor! And oh! He cares for the environment so much. He's got three rhinos with him!"

I stand corrected. BUT THEY'RE WEARING SUNGLASSES!!!!

"Well, now I know who I'M voting for," Mr. Pumpernickel said, putting his arm around his wife. "I never liked that other guy anyway. He's a complete..."

"DEAR!"

"What did I say?" Mr. Pumpernickel asked, confused.

"Nothing," Michael said. "Which is what I said."

"No, Michael," Mr. Pumpernickel said sternly. "YOU were about to say something terrible. I was about to say..."

"THE SAME THING!" Michael snapped. He was starting to miss his room, even though it was pretty lonely up there. *At least I have my toys...*

"I just don't know what's gotten into you, lately," Mr. Pumpernickel said, awkwardly putting his arm around Michael again. "Your mother and I just are worried about you. It's all we can think about. Right, dear?"

"Did you know that one of those news anchors is dating Jerry?" Mrs. Pumpernickel asked. "She doesn't deserve him."

"No she doesn't," Mr. Pumpernickel agreed. "Michael, we want what's best for you."

"Then why do you keep me locked in my room?!?!" Michael asked. "Is that what's best for me?"

"Certainly not," Mr. Pumpernickel laughed. "But it DOES give your mother and I more alone time!" he winked.

"Dear!" Mrs. Pumpernickel gasped, punching her husband on the shoulder. Suddenly, they locked eyes and began giggling. Michael had never heard his dad giggle before. It was creepy.

"Son, please go to your room," Mr. Pumpernickel said, not taking his eyes off his wife.

"Awww gross, Dad!" Michael said, disgusted. He covered his face with his hands and vowed to never leave his room again.

"What?" Mr. Pumpernickel asked, turning to face Michael. "Your mother and I were going to watch 'Wild Animals in the Wild' together. We haven't done it in a while."

Whatever, Michael thought in a typically sullen teenage way. He looked back at his parents, but they were already ignoring him as they cuddled up near the TV. And then Michael thought the last thing you're supposed to think. Ever.

Could my life get any worse?!?! he wondered, getting up from the couch and heading toward the stairs.

Yes, yes it could. Because as he began climbing toward his room, he was too distracted to notice that the Harrington Twin's body was gone!

Math is the devil, Michael thought, as he sat at his desk, frustrated.

He'd been working on his homework for four hours already and he was only on problem two. And that was just because he'd skipped problem one! He usually sat on his bed, but since he kept sliding to the ground, he'd found it to be somewhat distracting and had moved to his desk.

How am I supposed to get work done around here? Seriously! They need to invent a piece of furniture that's specifically made for work. Aha! Maybe I can do that and I'll get rich! Then I won't have to do math!

Suddenly, the door to his room opened. Well, it would have opened if it hadn't been locked. Instead, whoever was on the other side was struggling to get in and wasn't happy about it. Not at all. Not at all.

"WHAT IS GOING ON? I HATE THIS PLACE!!!"

The door rattled violently, shaking everything in Michael's room. He sat at his desk, frozen, hesitant to get up. Michael knew exactly who was on the other side of the door, and he was too nervous to open it.

"WHY IS YOUR DOOR ALWAYS LOCKED? YOU'RE SO WEIRD, MICHAEL PUMPERNICKEL!"

One of Michael's Distant Galaxy figurines fell off of the bookcase, shattering on the floor. He gasped. The door continued to rattle dangerously on its hinges.

"That's the last straw!" Michael said furiously. Standing up, he kicked aside the broken pieces of the robot and opened the door. "Lucy!" he said, brightly. "What a pleasant surprise!"

It was Lucy Peterson, the Third Love model from Miss Dandelion and Ms. Jones' booth at Some Town Fashion week.

"It's not a surprise you dweeb, you knew I was coming," Lucy said, shutting the door. She sat down on his bed and folded her arms. "Let's just get this over with."

Suddenly, another leg of the bed broke and she toppled to the ground.

- CHAPTER 4 -

"WHAT HAVE YOU DONE?!?" she screamed.

Michael laughed silently to himself. *At least my bed tilts forward now, not to the side...*

"What are you laughing at?!?" Lucy asked, angrily.

"Nothing," Michael said, reaching to help her up. She slapped away his hand and sat down at the desk, leaving him nowhere to sit. Michael stood in the middle of the room awkwardly, twiddling his thumbs.

"Did you eat too many Choco Squares?" he asked.

"AHHHHHHHHHHHH!!!!!" Lucy screamed.

Michael looked at her, horrified. *She sounds like a cross between a mountain lion and a mountain lion who doesn't know how to roar...*

"You don't ask a girl that kind of question," Lucy said, exasperated.

So THAT'S why I don't get any dates, Michael decided. *Although being locked in my room all the time has given me a lot of time to update my online dating profile. You'd think there would be a LOT more takers. Then again, maybe people don't like long walks on the beach anymore?*

"Have you finished your math homework yet?" Lucy asked, looking for it on his desk. Now 15, and in 10th grade, Lucy was Michael's weekly math tutor. She wasn't particularly patient, but she was pretty. That was good enough for him.

"Ummm...."

"Don't tell me. You're on problem two."

Yep.

"And that's only because you skipped problem one."

Crap! How did she know?!?!?!

"Michael, you do this every week! You really need to try harder!" Lucy frowned, drawing a large 'x' over the entire page and handing him his homework.

"I DO try hard," Michael said angrily, snatching it from her. "I just don't get it!" He ripped the paper in frustration and threw the pieces to the ground.

"WHAT ARE YOU GOING TO DO NOW, MICHAEL PUMPERNICKEL?" Lucy shouted, throwing her hands in the air. "You just ruined EVERYTHING! You're going to fail!"

- CHAPTER 4 -

My goodness! She's so hot when she's angry, Michael sighed.

The math wasn't his biggest problem, although he didn't understand that at all. It was the feelings he had for Lucy. He hadn't been able to talk to Crispin in almost two years, but he still felt guilty liking someone else.

What if she's been waiting for me? he wondered. *What would she say if she knew I liked someone else too?*

But Crispin hadn't called or visited him. She hadn't even sent a secret message through birds. Not that he knew how to do that. Maybe she didn't either?

What if she's forgotten about me? he frowned. *But if she has, how will I ever forget about HER?*

"WELL?!?!?!" Lucy snapped, brushing her blonde hair out of her face.

"Umm..."

A knock on the door saved Michael. It was Miss Dandelion! She smiled at them as she walked in and started to sit down on the bed.

"DON'T!!!!" Michael and Lucy yelled in unison.

Startled, Miss Dandelion leaned against the doorframe. "What are you guys up to?" she asked.

Why does SHE have to be here? Michael groaned. Despite his crushes on Crispin and Lucy, he had never quite gotten over his first love.

"Michael is being stupid. He ripped up his homework," Lucy said, pointing to the paper on the ground.

"Oh, my," Miss Dandelion frowned. "Is this true?"

Michael hung his head. He didn't really need to say anything. It was kind of obvious.

"I'm SO disappointed in you!" Miss Dandelion said, coming over and standing next to Lucy. "Why ever did you do such a thing?!?!"

"I just got frustrated," Michael said, shrugging. He couldn't bear to look her in the eye. He also didn't want to look Lucy in the eye because she was still glaring at him and he was scared, yet strangely attracted to her.

"Now, Michael, that's no reason to rip up your homework! You just have to keep trying! You can do it!"

"I know," he said, sadly.

"But I can't say I don't understand how you feel," Miss Dandelion said. "I've been getting frustrated too."

"Why, what's going on?" Lucy asked, finally relaxing her death stare.

"It's not one thing really," Miss Dandelion said sadly. "I mean, I shouldn't even be upset. I finally got married to Ralph, the man of my dreams!"

Gross.

"But it's the little things. I know it's not his fault he lost his job at Hungry Woody's. He'd worked so hard to become assistant general manager. We didn't know it was going to close so soon! I still can't believe it!"

Hungry Woody's is closed? Michael thought, horrified. *I was wondering why Ralph was around so much. Nobody tells me anything! But wait...what happened to Crispin and her dad? Oh no! I hope they're okay. Well, at least Crispin. Okay, maybe her dad too. I don't know, I can't worry about everybody!*

"Then again, that new place, Black Orb, IS pretty cool, if you're into that kind of thing," Miss Dandelion shrugged.

"I'M into that kind of thing," Lucy said, smiling and twirling her hair.

"Lucy, you're too young to get in! It's a trendy nightclub!" Miss Dandelion said, sternly.

So she can get into the regular nightclubs, but not the trendy ones? Michael wondered.

"But now we're living here at Ralph's parent's house, and I guess it's just not how I imagined things, you know?" Miss Dandelion sighed.

"It's going to be okay," Lucy said, giving her a reassuring smile. "Where is Ralph, anyway?"

"Oh, he's downstairs in the basement, I think," Miss Dandelion said. "Last I saw him, he was going down there with a stool, some paper and a rope. He looked depressed."

"WHAT?!?" Michael yelled.

Usually in books and movies when someone has those materials it means they're going to do something bad. Like potentially life-changing bad.

Miss Dandelion and Lucy looked at him like he didn't belong. But it was HIS room. HIS bed. HIS creepy blood stain. Back-up. HIS bed, NOT his bloodstain. Whatever. You know what I mean.

"I mean, like, aren't you worried about him? You know, and stuff?" Michael asked. "That doesn't sound good."

"Of course, Michael," Miss Dandelion said. "I just told Lucy that."

"But aren't you worried he'll do something stupid he shouldn't do? Something dangerous?" Michael asked, prepared to go save his brother's life.

"Not really," Miss Dandelion shrugged. "He said he was going to fix one of the light fixtures. I don't know what the rope and paper were for though."

I hope I don't either! Michael thought, heading toward the door. He ran out of the room as fast as he could, trying to get to the basement before it was too late!

When Michael opened the door to the basement, he couldn't see a thing. It was pitch black. And eerily silent.

That's not good, Michael thought, stepping forward into the darkness.

Unfortunately, the Pumpernickel's basement was much like other basements, and it had a long set of stairs leading to the ground. Not looking where he was going, Michael painfully fell down this long set of stairs.

THUMP! THUMP!

In case you were wondering, every staircase in the Pumpernickel household is long. They have an extremely tall, but narrow, house. Some people like that.

"MY LEG! MY ARM! MY HEAD! MY HAIR! MY FAVORITE SHIRT!" Michael was lying at the bottom of the staircase, shouting at the top of his lungs.

"Michael, is that you?" a voice asked from somewhere in the darkness.

"Ralph?" Michael said hopefully. If it was his brother, then it would mean he wasn't dead!

"What are you doing?" Ralph asked. "Are you just picking different parts of your body and screaming about them? Besides your favorite shirt, of course."

"My favorite shirt IS a part of my body," Michael said defiantly.

"That's true, you never wash it," Ralph chuckled. "What happened?"

"I FELL DOWN THE STAIRS!" Michael shouted. "Didn't you hear me?"

"I was wondering what that was," Ralph shrugged. "But I couldn't see what happened because it's dark."

"I know!" Michael said, frowning as he realized he wasn't going to get the attention he wanted. "What are

YOU doing down here, anyway? Miss Dandelion said you came down here with a stool, a rope and a piece of paper! I thought you were about to do something bad!"

"What?" Ralph asked, confused. "The stool was for me to sit on, the rope was so I could fix the light fixture and the piece of paper was so I could write down my thoughts. Nothing bad about that as far as I know. It's a free country."

"But it's still dark!" Michael said, sitting up.

"Way to state the obvious," Ralph laughed.

"I mean, you didn't fix the light fixture! I thought that's why you came down here?"

"I came down here because I'm depressed. I was going to write down my thoughts, but to do that, I had to fix the light fixture!"

"But you didn't."

"That's because I couldn't see to fix the light fixture!" Ralph said, rolling his eyes.

"So let me get this straight," Michael said. "You came down to the basement with a stool, a rope and a piece of paper because you're depressed."

"That's right."

"So you sat on the stool to write down your feelings, but couldn't see because you couldn't see to fix the light fixture?"

"I guess so," Ralph said.

"Then why didn't you use the flashlight that's right next to you on the ground?"

"The what?"

Ralph frowned, picking up the flashlight and turning it on. Suddenly, they both started laughing. And once they started, they found they couldn't stop. Michael walked over and sat down on a stool next to his brother.

"I guess there was already a stool down here too, wasn't there?" Ralph chuckled.

"It looks like it," Michael said.

"Thanks for sitting with me, Michael," Ralph said.

"What?" Michael asked.

"Thanks for just being here. For listening. I really need someone to talk to."

"But what about Miss Dandelion?" Michael said, frowning. "You guys are married now. Not that I was invited to the wedding because I had to stay in my room."

Ralph smiled. "Hey, that wasn't MY fault! I said we should have it in the backyard so you could look out your window. Alice wouldn't go for it though."

"It's alright," Michael said. "Mom wouldn't have let me wear my favorite shirt anyway. What's the point?"

The reception is the point! I can't believe Ralph had a triple chocolate, hot fudge, brownie chunk Oreo, M&M, Reese's cake. Even Prometheus got to have some! That's not even fair!

They sat in silence.

"So what's this I hear about Hungry Woody's closing?" Michael asked. "What happened?" He was never very good at silence.

"I don't know," Ralph said. "We were doing so well too! It came out of nowhere."

"I think I know who's behind it," Michael said.

"You do?" Ralph asked, confused. "Who?"

"Lord Piper," Michael said quietly.

The change in Ralph was instantaneous. "Don't get me started on all your imaginary friends!" he said angrily. "I just opened up to you and this is how you're going to treat me? I'm tired of all this stuff about talking animals and some evil plot to take over the world. Look at you. It's ruined your life! You're eleven, you shouldn't be acting this way."

"Actually, I'm thirteen, now..."

"Whatever. That's exactly my point!" Ralph said. "You've spent so long living in some made-up world that you missed two whole years of your life!"

"But it isn't made-up!" Michael said, beginning to get frustrated. "You saw it! You talked to Grohill!"

"I don't know what I saw, Michael," Ralph snapped. "But I DO know what's real! I lost my job and now Alice and I have to live here with you. And even though she says she supports me, I can't help but think she's disappointed. Sometimes, I worry she regrets marrying me!"

Michael counted to ten to control his anger. "Of course she doesn't regret it, Ralph. She told me."

"Wait, she did?" Ralph asked hopefully.

"Well, sort of, but that's not the point," Michael said, waving his hand. "The point is that she loves you and you're together. That's all that matters."

"I guess you're right," Ralph sighed.

"But that doesn't make the threat of Lord Piper any less real!" Michael said urgently.

"There you go again..." Ralph frowned.

"No, I'm SERIOUS, Ralph!" Michael said angrily. "Just think about it. How else can you explain Jerry Mudwater's rise to power?"

"He's a good businessman? I don't know."

"Exactly!" Michael said defiantly.

"What?"

"No, I mean exactly!" Michael said. "He's NOT a good businessman. He's just a guy who worked at Animal Control. I think Lord Piper is using him."

"Why should I believe you?" Ralph asked. "You haven't been outside in years. Things are fine. GREAT even. At least for most people... You went on and on about those Piperleaf necklaces, but they aren't dangerous. In fact, they're so popular they put Third Love out of business!"

"I didn't know," Michael said softly.

"Of COURSE you didn't know!" Ralph shouted. "You're too caught up in your own fantasies to live in the world around you! There are people out here who have REAL problems! People who NEED help! People like Moe. Did you know they never found his body after the big prison break a few years ago?"

"He's out there, Ralph," Michael said reassuringly. "I can feel it."

"You don't know that," Ralph said, a look of despair on his face. "He was my best friend, Michael. No one can replace that. I don't think I'll ever be the same."

"Ralph? Is that you?" Miss Dandelion asked. It sounded like she was at the top of the stairs, but honestly, it was kind of hard to tell. She probably was though because that made the most sense...

"It's me, Alice," Ralph said. "I'm down here with Michael."

"Why are you guys in the dark?"

"I couldn't fix the light because...oh, never mind," Ralph sighed. "What's going on?"

"I was wondering if you wanted to get some ice cream?" she asked. "I thought it might cheer you up."

"Sure," Ralph said. "Ice cream can't make the pain go away, but it IS awesome. Are you coming, Michael?"

"Michael has to do his homework," Miss Dandelion said. "Lucy says so."

"IF YOU RIP UP YOUR HOMEWORK AGAIN, I'LL RIP OFF YOUR HEAD!" Lucy shouted from somewhere in the house.

"She's kidding," Miss Dandelion chuckled uneasily.

Man, do I love her, Michael thought. *She's feisty!*

He sighed, following Ralph up the stairs. When he got to his room, he sat down at his desk and stared blankly at the new set of problems Lucy had prepared for him. Suddenly, the locks on his door began to click!

Who's doing that? he wondered.

When Michael woke up, he was chained to the underside of his bed...

Just kidding, that's ridiculous! We both know his bed is broken. That's not even possible! He was chained to the underside of his DESK! There! That makes WAY more sense, doesn't it?

Of COURSE it does! You're welcome.

How in the world did I get here? Michael wondered, attempting to sit up. Or sit down, depending on how you look at it. *What happened?*

The chains wouldn't budge. That's what happened.

"Cheese straws!" he said angrily. *It's dark under here. What the hey is going on?*

At age 13, Michael wasn't afraid to admit he was still afraid of the dark. After all, the dark was a lot scarier than most things. Like admitting his own personal failure of still being afraid of the dark. That was a breeze!

Michael hated the dark. He really, really hated it. And that's why being chained to the underside of a desk was so bad. It was dark under there! Really, really dark.

All I did yesterday was watch TV with my parents, right? he thought, hoping the chains would just break on their own. *And then I did my math homework! Okay, well, I sort of didn't do my math homework but...holy crow! Did Lucy do this to me?!?!?!*

He thought back to what he remembered from the day before. *No, she went to get ice cream with Ralph and Miss Dandelion. No one does mean things right after they eat ice cream. That's just plain wrong!*

Suddenly, he became hungry. *But what if she did do this? Does this make her even MORE attractive?*

Michael was thinking so hard he didn't hear the man call his name. Or begin to sing. He didn't even hear the footsteps as they approached the desk.

"Michael? Little dude? Maybe slightly big little dude? Where ARE you?"

The man, clean shaven and wearing a finely-pressed suit, looked completely out-of-place in Michael's room. You'd think he would have had a lot of time to clean it, but that just wasn't the case. Michael's room was filthy.

"If I can't find you, I'm going to be in like really big trouble. This is my first day so, you know, be nice and stuff," the man said nervously as he stepped over a giant puddle of dried blood. "I want this to work out! Your parents pay really well."

Michael still couldn't decide if Lucy locking him up was a good thing, or a bad thing. Surely, she couldn't expect him to do his math homework under here, could she? *Well, maybe,* he thought. *She's crazy!*

Confused, the man scratched his head. Michael wasn't in plain sight, THAT much was obvious. So where was he? The man thought about where HE would hide if he were Michael. Since a lot of his ideas wouldn't work because they weren't in the jungle, he looked over at the desk and smiled.

"I get it bro! I'd hide there too. But I don't think I'm that scary. I'm wearing a suit and guys in suits are always nice, law-abiding citizens. You can trust me, I promise."

(Although, if Michael DIDN'T trust him, the promise wouldn't have meant much...)

The man walked over and picked up the desk. "Gotcha," he said, smiling.

Michael screamed. Not only had he been completely absorbed in his thoughts, but the man's actions had been wildly unexpected. I mean, who does that kind of stuff? Since Michael screamed something we can't print, we'll just pretend he said this. It's a family book, after all-

"GOLLY GEE, SIR. YOU SURE SCARED ME! PLEASE DON'T DO THAT AGAIN!"

That's not what I said, Michael thought.

(You don't get a vote, it's MY book!)

The man was surprised too! He'd thought Michael might be under the desk, but he didn't expect him to be chained to it. He was so shocked, he dropped it back down.

"GOLLY GEE, SIR. YOU SURE SCARED ME! PLEASE DON'T DO THAT AGAIN!"

Michael was still screaming and now the man was too. He'd dropped the desk on his foot!

"WHOA THIS DOESN'T FEEL GOOD LIKE AT ALL! WHOA! OUCH! OH WOW, WHOA! OUCH! OUCH! OUCH! WHOA!!!"

Fortunately, for Michael, the chains unexpectedly broke when the desk hit the ground.

"HEY! THERE YOU ARE!" the man said. "What's happening, bro?" He put out a hand for a high five.

It was not returned.

BORIS? Michael thought, horrified. He looked the stranger up and down. Despite a poor attempt at masking his appearance, the man was very clearly the bass player. Michael was not pleased.

Not that he didn't like the guy. I mean, he really did, at least before Boris betrayed everyone and started working for Lord Piper. That kind of changed things.

But if Boris was there, it meant that Michael had another nanny. And if he had another nanny, well...that wasn't awesome. He didn't want to have to accidently let Boris kill himself. He hadn't even gotten away last time! He'd just woken up chained to a desk! Not even his bed which would have been more comfortable!

Boris smiled at Michael, hi-fiving himself and running his hand through his close-cropped hair.

What is he wearing anyway?!?! Michael frowned. *I have better costumes on Halloween. Like that parrot one I did a few years ago. I can't believe Ralph wouldn't let me stand on his shoulder. He ruined EVERYTHING!*

"I'm umm...Rupert?" Boris said uneasily. "I'm your new...umm...whatever." He chuckled and held out a hand to help Michael up. Instead, Michael helped himself up and Boris hi-fived himself, running his hand through his close-cropped hair. Again.

I really wish he would stop doing that. I know who he is. This is just silly. I think I'll go ahead and tell him.

"I know who you are," Michael said. "You're...."

WOOOOOO!!! WOOOO!!!!! WOOOO!!!!!!

The sound of a train whistle shook the room.

Say whatttttt? We don't have a train at our house! Or, near our house. Or, probably even in this town. I don't really know.

WOOOOOO!!! WOOOO!!!!! WOOOO!!!!!!

"Oh, sorry man, that's my cell," Boris said, silencing his phone. "It's a reminder to tell me to come to work. I'm early! Bonus time!" He was grinning from ear to ear.

"Yeah, maybe," Michael mumbled. *What was I about to say?* There was a ringing in his ears. *Oh yeah!* "I just wanted to tell you that I know who you are. You're..."

HONK!!! HONK!!!!! HONK!!!!!!

The sound of a giant tractor-trailer interrupted him.

"There I go again," Boris laughed, pulling his phone back out. "That reminder is to tell me that I need to take you to school! Come on, dude, let's go!"

Michael froze in his tracks. "I get to go to school?!"

"Well yeah, bro, school's kind of an important thing. It helps you get ahead in life. And when you're ahead, you're not behind. And when you're not behind, you're in front. And when you're in front, you're awesome."

He started to unlatch the locks on Michael's door. Which, you know, begs the question of how he got into the room, but I suppose that's for another day.

See? We've wasted a LOT of time already.

"But I'm not allowed to go to school," Michael said, shaking his head sadly. "I haven't been in like two years. They just send my homework by mail and then I finish it and send it back by mail. It's not a perfect system, but it works. I usually get a late grade, but it's not my fault."

"And, done! Lock number fifteen! It looks like we'll make it to school after all," Boris said, ignoring him. "Do you have all your stuff? Do you need to like, bring that chain with you?"

What?!?! NO...I don't even know how this got here.

"Totally up to you," Boris said, smiling. "I'm not sure what the 'kids' are into these days."

"I guess so?" Michael said, scratching his head. *WAIT!!!! What the hey...*

"Works for me, dude! It's kind of punk, but I like that look on you," Boris said, giving Michael a thumbs up. "Since you haven't been to school in a while, you need to establish that you're dangerous early on. It will help you let your classmates know who's boss."

"But I'm not the boss," Michael said. "I was tied to my desk while I was awake and I don't even remember it."

"Well, then it will help you with the ladies!" Boris grinned, motioning for Michael to go through the door. He put his hand out for another hi-five, but stopped and ran his hand through his close-cropped hair.

"I doubt it," Michael sighed. "I've had a lot of women problems recently. I haven't even heard from my girlfriend in two years."

"Me neither," Boris frowned, before realizing he'd given away too much. "Then if it can't help you with your classmates, or the ladies, then it can help you with math!" He motioned for Michael to go through the door. Again.

"Maybe," Michael said, hanging his head. "But I don't think Lucy would like that..."

"JUST LEAVE IT HERE AND GO THROUGH THE DOOR! WE HAVE TO GET TO SCHOOL!!!" Boris yelled, throwing the chain to the floor, his face turning red.

"What?" Michael asked, confused. He'd already forgotten what 'it' was. "Sure," he said, shrugging and walking down the stairs.

Boris gritted his teeth and sighed. He didn't want to get too angry and blow his cover.

When they got outside, Michael was dumbfounded. In an attempt to disguise his van, Boris had painted it green. It still looked like a lobster. It actually still said 'Cool Lobsters' on the side. It was just green instead of red.

"Wow, great car," Michael said, trying to get Boris all excited so he would confess.

Boris' eyes lit up, but then he clenched his fists and shook his head. "Oh yeah man, this old thing? Second hand. I got it from this cool cat down at the pawn shop. He said he knew you."

"Really," Michael laughed. "What was his name?"

Boris frowned. "Well, I can't tell you that. All transactions are confidential, after all. But he DID say he was sorry for doing the wrong thing and that he's going to do the RIGHT thing from now on. The fox tricked him into thinking he could help his band get big. Dumb, right? But then he realized he was being selfish and came back home. Kind of a weird message, I guess. Super nice guy though."

Michael smiled. "Are you sure that guy isn't you?"

"Positively positive, bro," Boris said, looking longingly at the car.

"And you met him where exactly?" Michael asked.

"The pawn shop, super nice guy."

"And did you get the snake there too?"

"No way man, I got her on a peace keeping expedition to Africa with my band and the prime minister. I rescued her from the horrors of the wild. You wouldn't believe the things I saw. It's a crazy world out there."

"Aha!!" Michael said triumphantly. "You never mentioned a snake before."

"Ahh...yeah about that," Boris said, realizing he'd screwed up. "I don't have a snake."

"I see one through your window."

"No, you don't."

"Yes, I do."

"No, I don't think you do."

"I really do."

"Are we going to do this all day?"

"I certainly hope not."

"Okay, good."

"Hey, you don't have to hide anymore," Michael chuckled, happy to have the old Boris back. "I...

THUMP! THUMP! THUMP! THUMP! THUMP! THUMP! THUMP! THUMP! THUMP! THUMP!

Hey, that sounded exactly like when I fell down the stairs!!! Or when the Twin did!!!

"Jumping Jehoshaphat, look at the time!" Boris said, tapping at his fake fancy watch. "My alarm's telling me we're late! We've missed the announcements already."

"Well, that's no loss," Michael muttered to himself.

"Let's go!" Boris said, picking Michael up and throwing him through the window of the van.

Taco salad, THAT HURT! Michael thought angrily.

"And if you do happen to see a snake in here, don't worry about it. I don't have one, so it's probably not real."

Whatever, Michael sighed, looking out the window. Even though he had been locked in his room for two years, he finally had hope - he was going to school!!!!

When Michael got to school, his whole world was flipped upside down. So much had happened while he was gone, he barely recognized the place!

Man, I'm really the glue around here, he thought, smiling to himself. *How did they even function without me?*

In fact, a lot HAD changed at Some Town Primary School. He wasn't lying! Most of his old 'friends' were gone. Jasper had failed a grade and transferred. Principal Goodburn had even moved on to become superintendant!

There were some new faces too. In Goodburn's place, was an irrationally boring person of no relevance to this story. And instead of Grumpy Old Ms. Jones, the other, potentially non-dead Harrington Twin had become his math teacher. Bad news bears. Seriously.

But the thing that made Michael MOST upset was the change in Tommy Snaggletooth. Angry from all of the years of bullying, Tommy had become the NEW bully. And to be honest, well, he wasn't really too bad at it. You know, being bad and stuff. It was a gift.

"Who's that, your babysitter?" Tommy snickered, as Michael walked into the room.

"Genius, Tommy," Michael said. "Really original. We should call you barbecue chips."

"What?" Tommy asked, confused. He winked at Michael and flexed his suddenly bulging muscles. All of the girls in the class sighed.

Disgusting. Michael thought, shaking his head.

"It's because a lot of barbecue chips are called 'original style.' It makes sense." He stuck out his tongue.

"Stick out your tongue at me like that, dweeb, and I'll make sure you can never taste chips again! Barbecue OR original!" Tommy growled, getting up from his desk.

Boris quickly moved in between them.

"You're pathetic, Pumpernickel," Tommy chuckled. "I hope you're ready for the test today. And you better be, because I've been getting bad grades without you."

"That's ENOUGH!" the Harrington Twin said, entering the room.

Michael shuddered. This Twin looked exactly like the guy who had fallen down the stairs. Well, except he wasn't covered in blood and hopefully, not carrying a knife.

"Snaggletooth is right," the Twin said, picking up a stack of papers. "You have a test today, and I mean, a BIG one. This could very well determine your course in life. Will you be a success?" he asked, glancing at Tommy and smiling. "Or, will you be dead?" he chuckled, sneering at Michael.

The room was silent.

"I mean, or will you be a failure," he said, coughing into his hand before starting to pass out the tests. "Before we begin," he said. "I have a song I would like for us to sing together. It's called, 'The Very Angry Fox Song.' Don't be shy, together, now!"

"But we don't know the words!" Michael frowned.

"Then I suggest that you learn them!" The Twin snapped. "This is a very important song I think you need to hear. It's very...instructive."

"Will it give us the answers to the test?" Tommy asked, hopefully. "Because if so, I think Michael should have to go outside. He hasn't been here like the rest of us."

"Oh no," the Twin chuckled maliciously. "Of everyone in the room, I think HE needs to hear this the most! Michael, I dedicate this song to you..."

"There once was a fox so kind and so fair

He had friends and fans everywhere

They worked really hard on his wonderful plan

To defeat the cowardly boy who ran

But this little boy, he dared to defy

The lovable fox, oh so hard did he try

What he didn't know is that with every breath

He came that much closer to imminent death

The fox would not stand for the boy's disregard

Of the plan that many had worked on so hard

And he gave a warning to his little friend

To give up and surrender his life in the endddddd!"

He's not terrible, but that was creepy, Michael thought. *Why did he say that I needed to hear it most of all? Now I'm going to be humming through the whole test!*

(Come on, Michael. You're the boy, and...)

The Twin smiled and crossed his arms, evidently pleased with himself. When the class didn't applaud he erupted. "CHEER FOR ME NOW! I WROTE THAT MYSELF, YOU FOOLS!" He clapped his hands together until they were raw.

Michael did his best to appear excited as he walked to the back of the room and sat down at an empty desk. Boris stood awkwardly behind him, reciting his multiplication tables, in case HE had to take the test too.

"Now, who's this?" the Twin asked, raising an eyebrow. "You're not allowed outside help."

"He's NOT outside help," Michael said, embarrassed. He's...um..."

"A babysitter, perhaps?" the Twin asked, smirking.

Tommy Snaggletooth snickered.

"CAN IT, SNAGGLETOOTH!!!!!"

"Pardon me, sir," Boris began. "If I may add, I'm not what you would call a babysitter. I'm more of a..."

"I don't care what you are," the Twin snapped. "You're not on my roll. You must leave immediately." The rest of Michael's class had stopped taking their tests and were now staring at him.

"Now wait a minute, bro," Boris said, running his hand through his close cropped hair. "Michael's parents and I cleared this with Principal Downflower this morning. She said Michael was allowed to come back to school as long as I came too. I don't see why that's a problem?"

"You don't?" the Twin whispered, getting close to Boris' face. "Could it be because Michael Pumpernickel is a troublemaker? A criminal?"

"He's NOT a troublemaker and he's NOT a criminal!" Boris said angrily, pushing the Twin aside. "Are you, Michael?"

They turned to Michael's desk. He was gone! Panicking, Boris ran out of the room. So far, he was a below-average nanny.

"MICHAEL! BRO! DUDE! LITTLE MAN! WHERE ARE YOU?"

The Twin's laughter rang down the hallway. Tommy Snaggletooth poked his head out of the door. "Hey, Michael! I took your test for you! You probably want to go ahead and move your things back to sixth grade. They've been saving a desk for you!"

Boris ran by the classroom again, throwing a lunch tray at Tommy's nose. Tommy crashed to the floor, screaming in pain.

"That's for like, being lame, man!" Boris yelled. Chuckling to himself, he stopped to assess the situation. Where WAS Michael?!?

He wasn't in the art room hiding in the pottery kiln. He wasn't in the music room hiding in the tympani. He wasn't even in the lunch room eating someone else's food! Boris had checked there six times just in case.

"Where IS this guy?" he wondered, scratching his head. "Oh wait..." he laughed, racing out to the playground.

One of the kindergarten classes was having recess, but that wouldn't stop Boris from looking around. The bass player pushed a five-year-old out of the slide, and began to crawl inside. Just as he suspected, he found Michael halfway up, curled into a ball.

"Hey, Michael, dude! You've got to come out, man. It's SUPER cramped in here," Boris said, slipping back down to the bottom. "I don't think I can make it up there, so you're going to have to come here. Can you do that?"

Michael shook his head. After two years of anticipation, his return to school had become a nightmare. Crispin wasn't even there!

"Nah, I get it, bro! That Snaggletooth kid has it coming, and I'm not even sure what IT is yet. But you can't hide all day. It's kind of compromising for us to be in here together."

A teacher started to bang on the side of the slide. "WHO'S in there?" she yelled, her high pitched voice echoing off the walls. "Did I see an adult go in the slide? Is this the janitor again? I warned you! Your probation officer isn't going to be very happy about this!"

"Michael, seriously!" Boris said anxiously, slipping toward the bottom again. "We're in big trouble here. This is a slippery slope."

Literally.

"HEY, OLD MAN! WHY DON'T YOU STOP TALKING AND KEEP SLIDING! WE DON'T HAVE ALL DAY! RECESS IS ONLY TWENTY MINUTES!!!"

Boris looked up and saw a very mean-looking kindergartener glaring at him from the top of the slide. The kid had a Mohawk and was wearing a tie-dye shirt.

"Listen, punk," Boris said angrily, doubling his climbing efforts. "I'm coming for you!" The Mohawk kid stuck out his tongue. The bass player growled and kept climbing.

"The Resource Officer is ALMOST HERE!" the teacher said, frantically banging on the side of the slide. "He just had to clean up some pudding in Principal Downflower's office. Not sure how it got all over her couch. There weren't even any kids in there! What a mess!"

"MICHAEL!" Boris said. "We have to get out of here, man!"

"I'M COMING DOWN!" the tie-dye kid sneered.

"Oh no, you're not!" Boris snapped. The tie-dye kid chuckled and walked away.

"Thank goodness," Boris said, extending a hand for Michael. As usual, Michael ignored him and Boris ran his fingers through his close-cropped hair. He's going to go bald if he keeps doing that.

Suddenly, the tie-dye kid reappeared, jumping toward them at full speed.

"WEEEEEEEEEEEEEEEEEEEE!!!!!" he yelled as they shot out the end of the slide. They crashed to the ground, taking the teacher with them.

"AHHHHHH! You ARE an adult!" she screamed, pushing Boris off of her. "NOW you're in trouble! Wait until the resource officer hears about this. I...wait a second..."

Boris looked up and realized it was one of Ms. Jones' friends. He grinned sheepishly.

"Boris? Is that you?!?!"

"Umm...maybe?" the bass player said. He was hoping his disguise would pay off this time.

"What are YOU doing here? In there? With my children?" The teacher was wide-eyed.

The tie-dye kid kicked Boris in the shin.

"WHOA THAT DOESN'T FEEL GOOD LIKE AT ALL! WHOA! OUCH! OH WOW, WHOA! OUCH! OUCH! OUCH! WHOA!!!" Boris yelled, clutching his leg.

"Now, Tommy, that wasn't very nice," the teacher said sternly.

Tommy? This one is mean too? Michael gasped.

The tie-dye kid stood up and started to cry. "I'm sorry, but he's SO mean!"

"Boris, why would Tommy say you're mean?" the teacher said angrily. "And you never explained why you were in the slide. And what's THAT?" she asked, pointing at Michael.

Seriously? Not 'who's that?' Or 'WHO'S THAT?!?!' You know, in the way you might say it if you're attracted to someone.

"That's Michael," Boris said. "I was in the slide trying to..."

SLAP!!!

"WHAT WAS THAT FOR?!?" Boris asked angrily.

The teacher was standing over him, her palm ready to hit him again. "WHERE HAVE YOU BEEN?!?!?" she said, gritting her teeth. "Margaret has been SO worried!! She quit her job to go look for you!!!"

"I just..." Boris grimaced, covering his face. He didn't know Ms. Jones had left the school. He hadn't talked to her since he'd gotten back. "Please don't hit me again," he whimpered.

"And another thing, I..."

RINNGGGGGG RINGGGGGG RINGGGGGGG

"Never mind, there's the bell," the teacher said, lowering her hand. "Recess is over."

"No, it's not," the tie-dye kid said. "That was the mean guy's phone!"

The teacher glanced at Boris. The bass player fought the urge to check his pocket.

RINNGGGGGG RINGGGGGG RINGGGGGGG

"That's probably just a reminder for him to take his drugs," Michael said, remembering something about Boris having allergies.

The teacher gasped. "First you abandon your loving girlfriend. THEN you climb into a slide with children! NOW you're on drugs? It's a good thing Margaret isn't here to see this! What do you have to say for yourself?"

"That I wish you would stop asking questions," Boris sighed. "You haven't even let me answer the first one."

"Let's talk about answers!" the teacher snapped, grabbing him by the collar and pulling him to his feet. Boris' phone fell to the ground.

RINNGGGGGG RINGGGGGG RINGGGGGGG

"TURN OFF YOUR STUPID PHONE!" she yelled.

By now, the entire playground was watching them. The tie-dye kid had a huge smile on his face.

"That was the bell, m'am," the school resource officer said, walking up. "Don't you need to go back to your classroom? Is this the guy you were telling me about?"

"This is him alright," the teacher said, releasing Boris. "Come on, children!"

The bass player coughed and clutched his chest. His shin still throbbed from the tie-dye kid's attack. They watched as the teacher led the class back into the school.

"Is he gone?" Boris asked, frantically looking around.

"He is NOW!" the kid said, kicking Boris in the OTHER shin before running away.

"You're DEAD! Do you hear me? You're DEAD!!!!" Boris yelled, chasing after him. The school resource officer tackled the bass player at the door.

"I heard you alright," the officer said sternly, pushing him to his feet. "And I think it's time you took your aggression somewhere else. Both of you." He glanced at Michael who was on the ground making a castle in the dirt. Aggressively, apparently. "LEAVE."

On the way back to the van, Michael looked up at Boris and smiled.

"What are YOU so happy about?" Boris grumbled, fiddling with his keys.

"At least we accomplished something," Michael laughed.

"What do you mean?" Boris asked. "We got kicked out of school. You probably failed your test. I think Margaret's friend is mad at me and my shins won't stop burning. What in the world could possibly be good about that? Are you seriously crazy right now, bro?"

"You finally admitted you're Boris," Michael said, grinning.

"Blast it, you're right!" Boris said, slamming his door as they got into the van. "But I had such a good disguise!" He ran his hand through his close-cropped hair.

"No, you really didn't," Michael said. "I've been trying to tell you. I've known the whole time."

"You mean I didn't have to shave my beard?" Boris asked, clearly upset.

"No, not really," Michael shrugged.

"And I didn't have to paint my van?!?!"

"Definitely not."

"Bummer..." Boris said. He was distraught.

They were silent for moment before Michael spoke up. "I forgive you, you know."

The bass player stared blankly at the windshield, the van idling loudly. "You do?"

"Sure," Michael said. "You made a mistake, I get that. We all have our moments!"

"It wasn't just a mistake though," Boris said, shaking his head. "I left Margaret! She quit her job because of ME! I was selfish! I betrayed all of you!"

"It doesn't matter now," Michael said."You're back. That's what we care about."

"But Margaret is GONE!" Boris sighed, closing his eyes. "Who KNOWS where she is! This is all my fault!"

"Listen, Boris, we have to move on!" Michael said, looking behind them.

"How can I move on when I've caused so much pain?" Boris wailed, hiding his face in the dashboard.

"No, I mean, we HAVE to move on," Michael said. "Early release carpool is starting and you're blocking the fire lane. You'll get a ticket."

The school resource officer was making his way toward them.

"Oh," Boris said, shifting into gear and turning onto the road. "Where should we go now?"

"To the Nervous Sleeve!" Michael said, exhilarated by his freedom.

"Man, this guy REALLY can't rap," Michael chuckled as they sped down the road. Not that he considered himself to be much of a rhythmic American poetry buff, but he did find it weird that Boris would listen to music that sucked. *He's a musician! Doesn't he have standards?*

"Yeah......" Boris said, pausing.

"What is it?" Michael asked, suddenly concerned. "Is there something wrong with the van? Are we going to die? Is it because of the music?" His heart began to beat quickly. He was about to see Crispin and NO ONE was going to take that away from him. Not even death!

"Yeah, this rapper is...ummm...me," Boris said, shaking his head.

"What?!?!" Michael asked, confused. "I thought the Cool Lobsters were a rock band?"

"They are," Boris sighed.

"Then what the hey is this?"

"Umm......yeah.....so like....you know how I maybe said that I was actually IN the Cool Lobsters? Yeahhhhh.....ummm...well, I'm not," Boris said quickly, covering his face.

"NO!" Michael said, shocked.

"It's true," Boris mumbled.

"No! I mean, NO, stop covering your face and watch the road! We're going to crash!!!"

"AHHHHHHHHHHHHHHHHHHHHHHHHHHH
HHHHHHHHHHHHHHHHHHHHHHHHHHHHHHHH
HHHHHHHHHHHHHHHHHHHHHHHHHHHHHHHH
HHHHHHHHHHHHHHHHHHHHHHH!" they screamed.

As Boris looked up, the car careened off the road, crashing into the front porch of a once regal house. When the dust settled, Michael poked his head through the shattered windshield and glanced around.

"Hey, cool! I recognize this place!" he said, excitedly. "We're here!"

They had landed right inside the headquarters of the Nervous Sleeve! Pretty convenient, although a tad structurally concerning. Michael looked over and saw that his grandfather's house had been torn down and replaced by a mattress store. *Those things are everywhere!* he thought, shaking his head.

The rest of the neighborhood wasn't in much better shape. All of the nice homes now had bars on their windows. One guy even had a moat with what looked like a dragon or something. Apparently, Jerry Mudwater's redevelopment hadn't hit the 'nice' part of town yet.

"My van. My van. My van. My van. My van. My van. My van. My van...." Boris stuttered.

"Stop trying to change the subject," Michael snapped, putting his hands on his hips. "So you're telling me you sold us out to Lord Piper because of a band you're NOT ACTUALLY IN?!?" He was furious.

Boris burst into tears. "I'm sorry I didn't tell you everything! I didn't tell ANYBODY everything. I was too ashamed, bro! I just couldn't say that I tried out for the Lobsters and was rejected. Or that I stalked the band and was given a restraining order. Or that I study every detail of their lives so I can live vicariously through them and tell their stories like they're my own. That's just not rad, man! It's not rad at all! What would people think of me?" He refused to get out of the van.

"That you were honest at least, holy crow!" Michael said, disbelievingly. "So Grumpy Old Ms. Jones doesn't know? You haven't told her?"

"No."

"And Ralph doesn't know?!?"

"Not yet."

"And I don't know?!?"

"I just told you."

"Oh yeah. Whoa...."

Michael was stunned. He almost felt sorry for Boris. *I mean, the guy just puts on a front to make people think he's cool. That sounds like middle school. That's MY job!*

"So what's with the van?" he asked.

"It's what I use to drive to their concerts. Cross-country," Boris shrugged. "The gas mileage isn't great."

"You go to EVERY concert?!?!?" Michael asked, amazed.

"Well, yeah. Otherwise, people would think I wasn't actually in the band!"

"Oh yeah..." *I'm hungry*, Michael thought. *Too much thinking.* "So hey, Boris, let's go inside the Sleeve and maybe you can tell everybody what you told me. I think you'd feel better."

He offered the bass player a hand. When Boris reached up to grab it, Michael pulled his hand back quickly and ran it through his medium-length hair.

"Gotcha!" he said, laughing.

Boris smiled and they went inside. Which was easy because they'd made a huge hole in the wall. Funny how that works.

"Where IS everybody?!?" Michael asked, confused. Stan's house was deserted!

"I don't know," Boris said, scratching his head. "I hope something bad didn't happen."

Michael's heart grew heavy. *Crispin...*he thought.

They walked through the mansion room by room, looking for a sign of struggle. They found one everywhere - it was a mess! The one thing they DIDN'T find was food. That made Michael mad.

"Did YOU do this?!?" he asked angrily, somewhat hoping that Boris had been a part of it so he would have a little more info.

"Me? What? Nah man," Boris said. "It could have been anybody. There's a lot of guys you know working for Lord Piper. Todd, Dapply, Chet, Tugley, Grohill...Mable even stopped by one time."

Michael kicked Wiggly Tom's computer in frustration. He thought for SURE if he was able to escape his parent's house that he'd be able to find Crispin and the others. Now, he felt like he was better off not knowing they'd been attacked. He felt helpless. And still hungry.

RUSTLE RUSTLE RUSTLE RUSTLE

"What was THAT?" Michael whispered extremely loudly. He'd never really been good at whispering...

"I don't know, home slice," Boris said, looking over his shoulder. "We better get out of here, though. Fast! It sounds like whoever trashed the place has come back for more!"

Or, it could be the police because we crashed a giant lobster into the front porch, Michael thought as they tip-toed toward the kitchen. *Either way, I'm doing one last cookie search.*

"I heard about your grandfather," Boris said as they dug through the pantry. "I'm really sorry, man. I know that's not cool and stuff."

"I was mad at my parents for so long," Michael said as he picked up something white from the ground and put it in his mouth. *Nuts! That's a piece of the wall...*

"And then what?" Boris asked, eating something brown he'd found on the floor. "Ah junk, man. Linoleum!"

"I just wasn't," Michael said, shrugging. "This whole experience, like, this whole thing with Lord Piper...I still don't know what to think about it two years later. The last time I talked to him, I really started to wonder if I had it all wrong. You know, like maybe he isn't super bad after all. That's what scares me."

SWISH SWISH SWISH SWISH

"It's getting closer!" Michael gasped. He spotted something with his name on it across the room and started to move. Boris pulled him back. "Whoaaa!" Michael said, angrily. "Holy crow, what are you doing? That has my name on it! It's MINE!"

Boris put a finger to his mouth and motioned for them to hide behind one of Poppy's cages. "Look!"

Michael gasped as Chet and Dapply entered the room.

SWISH SWISH SWISH SWISH

"Do you HAVE to make that swishing sound?" Dapply asked, agitated. "We'll NEVER find them with you making all that noise. You're giving me a headache, and I HATE headaches."

"Can it, Daniel. You know my new wind pants are more fashionable than anything YOU own. You're just jealous."

"I NEVER go out of style," Dapply said, clearly offended. "And besides. Purple and teal? Who WEARS that? The only thing worse is a green and white striped shirt with a blue collar."

*Wait a second...*Michael thought. *Did he just insult MY FAVORITE SHIRT?"*

"I can't believe we're doing this peasant work again," Chet said. "I thought Lord Piper had forgotten about the kid anyway."

"He didn't forget about him, that's ridiculous," Dapply chuckled, opening and closing the two cabinets that were still standing. "The reason he left him alone is so he'd be out of the way. Everything worked perfectly! That fool Goddard is gone. Jerry is in position. Goodburn is in position. Even Doogie. Now that the whole necklace thing has blown over, everyone thinks Lord Piper is just a businessman. Well, he is, but he's so much more than that."

"I really can admire his evilness," Chet agreed, as they moved into the next room. "It makes me want to sing, but that's just overdone."

"So true," Dapply said, nodding.

Somehow, the two villains hadn't thought to check behind the dog cage. Michael breathed a sigh of relief. "AHHHHHHHHHHHHHHHHHHHHHHHHHH....."

"TOO LOUD!" Boris whispered.

"Sorry," Michael said, frowning. He looked at the piece of trash again, but Boris pulled him back.

SWISH SWISH SWISH SWISH

"...and his plan about trying to ruin the lives of the monks from his old monastery? Priceless!" Dapply laughed, as they reentered the kitchen. "I had no idea that dump Hungry Woody's was owned by one of those guys. I can't believe Minotaur was going to play there. I'm so glad it's gone. What a complete joke, right? Unbelievable."

"No kidding, Donald. That cow gave me the creeps!" Chet chuckled, looking around. "Why did we come back in here again?"

"I think I saw a dog cage we didn't check. I wanted to be thorough. Lord Piper said he wants to bring in the kid so he can try out his new invention."

New invention? Even worse than the necklaces which appear to not have done anything at all? Blast!

"Michael, dude. We have to make a break for it," Boris said, as Dapply and Chet moved closer. "If we're caught that's it, man. Endgame. It will be much worse than being stuck at your parent's house, trust me."

"Okay!" Michael said, standing up and running for the door. He knocked Chet and Dapply to the ground, hoping to give Boris a chance to escape too.

"I didn't mean NOW!" the bass player yelled, chasing after him. "I mean, I did, but not now now. You know, like, LATER now."

Chet and Dapply quickly overcame their surprise.

"It's so nice to see you, Montgomery!" Chet said brightly, running up beside him.

"Don't you know my name yet?" Michael asked. He was out of breath.

"I'm bad with names, is that a crime?" Chet snapped, slowing down to Michael's pace.

"No, but that wind suit is!" Michael laughed. It was funny even though he was probably about to die.

SWISH SWISH SWISH SWISH

"WHAT DOES EVERYBODY HAVE AGAINST MY WIND SUIT? IT'S NOT THAT BAD!" Chet growled. He stopped in the middle of the hallway and looked down at himself. "SEE? IT'S WONDERFUL!"

"Thanks for stopping, big guy," Boris said, brushing past the otter and knocking him to the ground.

"Get up, you fool!" Dapply yelled, picking up Chet and running after Boris. "You don't want Lord Piper to do to you what he did to the Twin! He still hasn't forgiven him for the issue at the boy's house. That was a disaster!"

"LET GO OF ME YOU INFERIOR CREATURE!" Chet screamed, struggling in Dapply's grip. "I just want someone to appreciate my unique sense of style!"

"That would require you to have style!" Michael yelled, as they neared the front door. Or rather, front hole, since they'd crashed onto the porch. It was a bit drafty.

"So what's the plan?" Boris asked, picking up a lamp and throwing it at Dapply.

"I figured we'd take your car," Michael shrugged.

"Umm...Michael?" Boris said as they ran onto the front lawn. "What car?!?!"

Dern fern! Michael cursed, realizing his mistake.

"Hey, wait a second. If I remember correctly, Stan has a ton of motorized scooters in his garage!"

"I'm not even going to ask," Boris sighed, as they ran to the side of the house.

Thankfully, the garage was still intact. Boris and Michael quickly found the scooters and started them up, just as Dapply and Chet rounded the corner.

"You're not getting away, Pumpernickel!" Dapply snarled, standing in the entrance.

Michael looked around and saw the garage door opener on the wall beside them. Unfortunately, Chet saw it at the same time.

"Just leave it," Boris said. "Follow me!"

Yes, they're wearing helmets. Don't worry.

That's exactly the opposite of the plan I developed in my head! Michael thought. *Oh well...*

Chet dove for the button as Michael and Boris shot toward the door. Surprised, Dapply jumped out of the way, even though he wasn't near them. Chet yelled triumphantly as it began to close.

"WE'RE NOT GOING TO MAKE IT!" Michael yelled, glancing at Boris in desperation. They were only a third of the way to the door and it was already halfway down!

Unfortunately, much like the rest of the house, Stan's garage was extremely large. And long. Really long. And naturally, he kept his motorized scooters at the back.

Because where else would you keep them?

"ISN'T THIS RADIO WONDERFUL?" Boris shouted, bobbing his head.

That's not related to my comment at all, Michael thought, angrily.

The door was almost closed and they were only halfway there!

"We've got you now!" Chet said greedily, waiting for them to give up. He looked beside him and realized that Dapply was on the wrong side of the door. "At least...I'VE got you now!" he laughed, throwing his head back in celebration.

"BORIS, WE HAVE TO STOP!" Michael yelled.

They were almost there and the door had closed completely!

"I had no idea Stan listened to the Cool Lobsters!" Boris said, excitedly. "I just developed such a new respect for him. Wow!"

"BORIS, THIRTY FEET!" Michael yelled.

"HAHAHAHAHAHA...."- That's Chet laughing.

"This is my favorite song, too!" Boris said.

"TWENTY FEET!!!!" Michael yelled.

"I wonder if he has their new album? It's so experimental...."

"TEN FEET!" Michael screamed, bracing himself for impact. He never thought he would die young, but he'd at least hoped his life would flash before his eyes if he did.

No such luck.

"HOLD ON!!!" Boris yelled. "THIS IS IT!!!"

"ARE YOU CRAZY?!?" Chet gasped, jumping out of the way.

They hit the garage door with a bang, wood splintering in every direction. Boris hit first, shielding Michael from much of the blast. Since the bass player was so big, they barreled through with no problem, landing on the sidewalk at full speed.

"I wasn't sure that was going to work," Michael said truthfully as they sought to put as much distance between themselves and Stan's house as possible.

"Oh, really?" Boris asked. "Why didn't you just say something?"

Michael fought the urge to scream.

He's right, I should have said something. Instead, I yelled it. And instead of listening, he sang songs from the band he pretended to be in. He's TOTALLY right!

"It feels good to get out of there," Boris laughed, brushing a giant piece of plywood out of his hair.

Michael looked back and saw Dapply struggling to get free of one of the bushes. *So THAT'S what I hit when we went through the garage*, he thought.

"I don't think I could have taken another second of Chet's wind suit anyway," he chuckled.

"Now what?" Boris asked as Stan's house faded into the distance. "Not that I'm not up for joyriding, but I think these things only hold a charge for so long. Then we'll have to plug up."

"I know just the place!" Michael said, excitedly, remembering the paper he'd seen in the house. *It was a note with my name on it!* "To the Nervous Sleeve!"

"But we just left there?!?!" Boris said, skeptically, looking at Michael like he had three heads. Which would have been cool and maybe useful. We'll never know.

Which is too bad because...oh, never mind.

"Not 'Stan's house' the Nervous Sleeve," Michael said, smiling. "Hungry Woody's!"

"That place is closed!" Boris said, shaking his head. "They won't even be able to serve us food!"

"Oh, I think they'll be able to do that," Michael said. "And hopefully, more. Like answer a lot of questions. Come on!"

This time it was Michael's turn to speed ahead. Shocked and confused, Boris followed close behind him, hoping for their lives he was right.

Michael stood outside Hungry Woody's, second-guessing the magical piece of trash he'd found. The restaurant looked deserted!

"Ummm...should we knock?" he asked.

Boris shrugged. "I don't see why not. If there's no one here, then there's no reason to feel foolish for knocking."

"But if there IS no one here, then that's exactly WHY I should feel foolish for knocking," Michael said.

"What if I knock?" Boris asked, stepping forward.

Michael put his arm out to block him. "That's the same thing, just for you. We can't do that! It would be foolish, not to mention a tad ridiculous."

"Then what should we do?" Boris asked, running his hand through his close-cropped hair.

Suddenly, the door to Hungry Woody's opened.

"CHEESE AND CRACKERS!!!!!" Michael yelled, jumping ten feet into the air.

"We've got that, if you want some," Moe laughed, greeting them with a smile. "Wait a second...guys, you're HERE!" he said happily, pulling them into an embrace.

"You're crushing my face," Michael said. He was wedged between the two larger men.

Michael thought about his brother Ralph and the hard time he'd been having. Ralph would be overjoyed to hear that his best friend was alive and well!

"Quick, follow me," Moe said, ushering them through the door. The inside of Hungry Woody's was exactly how Michael remembered. Even the cow costume hung in the corner.

"You like that guy?" Moe asked. "We thought he helped create a little bit of atmosphere."

Atmosphere, my foot. SO CREEPY!

"Are you guys hungry?" Moe asked leading them through the maze of tables.

"Am I ever not?" Michael said, smiling.

"Of course," Moe chuckled. "Anyway, I can't wait to tell the others you're here!" Moe said, excitedly. "They've been so worried about you, Michael. You too, Boris."

"Me?!?!" Boris asked, confused. He looked at Michael. "Don't they know that I...."

"Betrayed us to Lord Piper because you wanted your band to get big? You changed your mind, our inside source told us. Maybe you can help us fill in the blanks about a few things?"

"But he's not even in a band," Michael muttered so Moe couldn't hear him.

"Just go with it!" Boris whispered. "With luck, we'll be eating a triple pickle, mutton glutton, big time burger within the hour!"

Or not...that thing was nasty, Michael thought. His stomach growled. *On second thought, I think I can manage.* He'd missed snack time at school and it had to be getting close to dinner. *This place brings back so many memories. Learning about Miss Dandelion and Ralph for the first time. Getting chased by Dapply. Seeing Crispin...Wait! Crispin!!!!*

"Moe, is Crispin here?" Michael asked, looking around excitedly.

Moe paused at the door and frowned. He turned around and put his hand on Michael's shoulder. "She's not," he said, his voice shaking. "We don't know where she is."

"WHAT?!?" Michael screamed. The only thing that had kept him going the last few years was the thought of seeing her again. Overwhelmed, he fell to the ground.

"Umm...bro?" Boris asked, looking uncomfortable.

"We haven't stopped looking, Michael," Moe said, kneeling down next to him.

"But where IS she?" Michael cried. "I don't understand! I thought she was with you?"

Moe sat down next to Michael. "When we broke out of jail and got back to the Sleeve, things got crazy. The three-legged cat and grumpy turtle blindsided us."

"Wait, you mean like they tried to kill you or something?" Michael asked.

"It was more than that though. Apparently, they'd been using you to try to get closer to Lord Piper," Moe sighed. He looked tired.

"Then what happened?"

"Some of us got away, but not before they took Tom and Crispin. The house was a mess so we came here to try to regroup. With Paul gone, Omar was the leading candidate to replace him, but some of the animals killed him during the night. I was eventually made leader, but not before those same animals left to join Lord Piper. Soon after, we received a letter from someone who's been helping us ever since. I guess they regretted their decision."

"It's all my fault, I should have been here," Michael said, wiping the tears from his eyes.

(You were kind of tied up though...)

"It's NOT your fault!" Moe said, defiantly. "We never should have left Crispin and the others alone with the cat. We had no idea what he was capable of."

"But I don't understand," Michael said, becoming angry. "Where did they take Crispin? And WHERE HAVE YOU GUYS BEEN?" He pushed Moe's hand off his back.

"You weren't there when I needed you. You weren't there when Crispin needed you! How can you say that you care when you let something like this happen?"

"Michael," Moe said sternly, his lips trembling. "Believe me, I miss them just as much as you do, and I'm still pretty new to this whole thing. I figured I would spend the rest of my life in that jail cell writing poetry. But I was given a second chance! We've looked everywhere for Crispin and Tom. All of us. We wanted to rescue you, but with that Twin hovering so closely, it was too dangerous. We hoped that you would break free and find us some day. That's why we left that note."

Some help THAT was, Michael thought, overcome with grief. He believed that Moe and the others had done what they thought was right, but Crispin was still out there. He had to find her...but how? What could he do?

"Let's go get some food," Boris said, trying to lighten the mood. He put out his hand to help Michael up, but Michael didn't move. Boris ran his hand through his close-cropped hair. Foiled again!

"He's right," Moe said, helping Michael up. "Let's go find the others."

"Finally..." Boris muttered.

They walked into the kitchen and were greeted by some familiar faces. Mable and Cephas were tending to something in the oven.

"I was wondering when you were going to come in!" Mable said brightly, giving Michael a hug. She turned to Boris and exchanged an awkward handshake.

(Even I felt awkward, and I wasn't there.)

"Who is that?" Cephas asked, feeling around for a pot on the top of the cooking surface. His hands came dangerously close to the burner.

"Who IS that?" Mable said sternly. "You know exactly who that is, you heard them in the other room."

"I can't be sure," Cephas said, smiling. "I'm blind!" He began to pour the contents of the pot onto the floor.

"WELL, GOLLY YOWSERS THAT HURTS!" a voice said from behind the island in the center of the room.

"Stan?" Michael asked, confused. He walked around and saw that Cephas had poured an entire pot of soup on his grandpa's (former) neighbor.

"Sorry, I didn't see you there!" Cephas chuckled, placing the pot back on the burner in the exact same spot as before.

"OOOOO you really sour my milk sometimes, Cephas Pumpernickel!" Mable said, grabbing a dish towel and whipping him in the back.

"Pumpernickel?!?" Boris asked. "You mean like Michael Pumpernickel?!?"

"Of course not, dear," Mable said, putting the towel on the rack and returning to the oven. "Animals don't have last names, that's just silly," she chuckled. "I just didn't know what to call Cephas when I'm angry at him, so I started using Michael's name. I hope that's okay."

"Umm...sure?" Michael said, shrugging. He was really disappointed to not have animal relatives. That would have been really cool. REALLY cool.

"This soup is cold," Stan said as he licked his fingers. "And bad. Is that hemlock?"

Moe's eyes grew wide. "Mable, what are you making?!?!" he asked, brushing past Michael to go check on Stan.

"Well, originally it was something to try to unclog the drain," Cephas said. "But we'll see if Stan dies in the next few minutes. If he doesn't, we've got ourselves a hearty dinner!"

"No we don't, you dropped it!" Mable scolded.

"Am I going to die?" Stan whimpered, pulling his sweater vest over his bulging stomach. It looked even more hideous when wet.

"Nah, bro!" Boris said. "I mean probably not."

"You're going to be fine, Stan," Moe said reassuringly, handing him a towel.

"So like, where's everybody else?" Michael asked, looking around. "Is this it?"

"Well you know about Crispin and Tom," Moe said, holding Stan as he began to cry. "The younger villagers like Sneaks and the Club are still with Lord Piper as far as we know. A lot of the animals left when Omar was killed. Even Poppy."

WHAT?!?!

Stan began to sob louder.

"Ruxiben is around here somewhere," Moe continued, patting Stan on the head. "Although I'm not sure where. Schumer is out on a reconnaissance mission to get news from the inside contact we mentioned."

"So what's up with this inside contact, bro?" Boris asked, pulling up a chair and sitting next to the pantry. He began taking out random food and eating it.

I want to do that! Michael thought hungrily.

"Well, like I was telling you before," Moe said, motioning for Michael to get him more towels, "we just got the letter a few weeks ago. It was addressed to 'The Leader of the Nervous Sleeve Organization Against Lord Piper.'"

"Kind of long winded," Michael laughed, taking off his shirt and handing it to Moe.

"No." Moe said, shaking his head. "Put it back on."

"But I couldn't find any towels!" Michael complained, shaking his shirt in Moe's face.

It was true, they were out of towels. But no one wanted to see that.

NO ONE.

"Fine..." Michael said, sighing. "But it's my FAVORITE shirt, so it would have been really helpful."

Boris laughed, shoving a whole sleeve of Mr. Sugar's Choco Squares in his mouth.

"Not helping, Boris," Moe said, clearly frustrated. "He may not know how to write a short letter, but the contact has proven to be really useful. It's how we know Lord Piper is up to something new."

"Yeah, a new invention," Michael said dismissively, inching his way toward the pantry.

"How do you know about that?" Moe asked. "Our contact said it hadn't been revealed yet."

"Oh, Chet and Dapply mentioned something about it," Michael said, snatching a tube of Choco Squares out of Boris' hands. He was hungry and that was serious business.

"Hey!" Boris said, angrily.

"Then they're getting cocky," Moe cringed, looking down at his damp shirt.

"But what should we do?" Michael asked. "We don't know what the invention is, or what it can do?"

"We can't do much of anything," Moe said, hanging his head. "Until we get some more information, we're stuck!"

"Then you'll be happy to know I've got news!" Schumer announced, bounding into the room.

Michael smiled. His old friend had snuck up on them once again.

"Schumer!" Michael said, dropping the Choco Squares and running over to greet the moose. Boris quickly grabbed the Squares off the floor and finished them.

"MICHAEL!!!" Schumer yelled, tackling his friend to the ground.

"Who IS that?" Cephas asked, confused.

Everyone paused and stared at him before they all started laughing. Even Mable, who took her hand off the dish towel and smiled.

"I'm ever so happy you're alive!" the moose cried.

"What's that note, Schumer?" Moe asked, checking Stan's pulse (he'd passed out) before walking over to them. "Or what WAS the note."

Whatever Schumer had brought had been ruined when he tackled Michael. Come on, Schumer. Priorities.

"Oh goodness!" Schumer said, dropping Michael with a thud. "It was the latest note from our contact!"

"And you just screwed it up? Nice one, home slice!" Boris laughed, leaning back and putting his feet on the counter. Mable knocked them off with her spoon.

"Why is HE here?" Schumer asked, pointing at the bass player. He was angrier than Michael had ever seen him.

"Schumer, we went over this," Moe said, standing in between them. "Boris made a mistake, but he acknowledged that he did the wrong thing. Don't we all deserve a second chance?" he said, glancing at Mable.

The mole nodded sadly.

"And anyway," Moe laughed. "It's not like we're all in a cutting-edge rock band, so there's no way we could understand what he was going through. I'm sure it was a VERY difficult decision. Let bygones be bygones though, whatever that means..."

Michael glared at the bass player, but Boris shook his head and put a finger to his mouth. Apparently, now was NOT the time for Boris to confess his playing status.

"I guess," Schumer said. "Although, I do play a mean pipe organ."

"THAT I would love to see," Boris laughed, absentmindedly putting his feet back on the counter again.

Mable growled at him.

"So what did the note say?" Moe asked, trying to decipher the pieces.

"Well, I always try to wait to read it when everyone's around," Schumer said. "But..."

"You never do!" Michael guessed, laughing.

"YOU GOT IT!" Schumer smiled.

They all breathed a sigh of relief.

"As you know, Lord Piper is trying to ruin the lives of the monks at the monastery where he grew up. We believe that Crispin's dad, the owner of Hungry Woody's, was one of these monks. Apparently, the mayor of Some Town may have been as well."

"But that guy was only 35!" Michael said, confused.

Everyone started at him.

"What?!?" he asked. "I keep up with local politics. I've had a lot of free time."

"Anyway," Schumer said, chuckling, "it appears that Lord Piper is ALSO trying to ruin the lives of the monks' descendants. So that could explain the age difference in who is targeted and stuff."

"That does explain it a little," Michael said. "But I don't understand what this has to do with Lord Piper's overall plan? The mayor's career was about to be tanked anyway due to his extracurricular activities in the office after hours."

"Wait, what are you talking about?" Moe asked. "I thought everyone hated him because he opposed the shopping mall that created all those jobs?"

"That too, but trust me, just wait," Michael said.

"Well, our contact believes that not only is Lord Piper trying to ruin the mayor's career because of his family connection, but also so he can..."

"Install Jerry Mudwater as mayor!" Michael gasped, suddenly remembering the press conference he'd seen on the news.

"Exactly," Schumer said, shaking his head. "The reason we haven't seen the effects of Lord Piper's plan yet is because his overall goal hasn't been accomplished. Once he takes over Some Town...well, we're all finished."

"Did the contact say anything about Lord Piper's new invention?" Moe asked. "The sooner we can figure out what it is the better."

"Not this time," Schumer said. "But he did indicate that there's reason to believe that the three-legged cat and the turtle are still alive."

"CRISPIN!" Michael said, hopefully. "Did he mention her?!?"

"Not by name," Schumer said sadly. "But he told me about a ferret who thinks he knows where they might be."

"A ferret?" Michael asked. "Do you think he meant Blinky? He was my former principal's pet. He was a bad character. I wouldn't be surprised if he's shacked up with Lord Piper."

"Well, I know Omar and Lieutenant Paul found the cat and turtle at your school so that makes sense," Moe said, scratching his head. "But where does Blinky think they're hiding?"

"He didn't say specifically," Schumer sighed. "But he gave me an address!"

"Rad, dude!" Boris said, between mouthfuls of Snappy's Colorful Rainbow Chips. "Where to?"

"Yeah, see that's the problem," Schumer frowned, picking up the scrap of paper again. "It was on here, and I can't remember what it said."

"Let me see it!" Cephas said, walking over.

"But you're blind?!?!" Boris frowned. "How can you read it if WE can't even read it?!?!"

Cephas winked. "Don't you worry about that, son." He picked up the piece of paper from the counter and held it close to his face. He squinted at the tiny letters and made a few noises to himself. "Yes...of course," he said.

"What is it?" Michael asked excitedly. "Do you know where it is? Can you find Crispin?!?"

"No," Cephas chuckled, handing it to Michael. "But I know what it says!"

"So we have an address," Michael said, staring at the slip of paper, "but we don't know where this place is. Should we be worried? I mean, anything could be waiting for us there. Literally anything. Monsters. Tigers. MORE monsters. I don't know about that."

"Nah, bro! Don't worry about it!" Boris laughed, shaking his head. "Even if it IS something scary, we can handle it! Is there anything we haven't overcome before?"

(That's the spirit!)

"Yeah," Michael mumbled. "Loads of stuff. Lord Piper's evil plan. The three-legged cat's evil plan. The death and defection of half of our friends. But I mean, besides that, nothing, I guess."

"Well, when you put it that way, it sounds bad," Boris frowned. "Now you're making ME nervous. I'd forgotten about all of that stuff."

"Are you guys sure you want to go to this address?" the cab driver asked, turning around to face them. "It's not in the greatest part of town."

"I'm not sure," Michael said. "But I think we're going there anyway."

"You bet we are!" Boris said, smiling. "Oh wait, dude, can we make a detour first?"

"Whatever you say, boss," the driver shrugged. "You guys pay me to take you around." He pulled over, waiting for them to tell him where to go to next.

This cab costs money? Michael thought, looking through his pockets. *My Sneaky Pete wallet is at home!*

"Don't tell him we don't have any money until it's too late," Boris whispered, looking very serious.

Michael made the motion of zipping his lips shut. Mostly, just because it felt like the right thing to do.

"Anyway," Boris said, clearing his throat, "I thought I should go visit your brother Ralph. You know, tell him and Alice that I'm back."

"I don't have a brother Ralph," the driver frowned.

"I'm not talking to you, I'm talking to him," Boris said, pointing at Michael.

"But I'M the one you SHOULD be talking to," the driver said. "I'm the one who's going to take you there."

"I know," Boris said. "And I was going to tell you, but not until I told Michael."

"Fine, just exclude me. I'm a cab driver. Who cares about me, right?" the driver sighed, shaking his head.

"I think it's a GREAT idea!" Michael said, giving Boris a thumbs up.

"You too?" the cab driver mumbled. "Doesn't anybody have any respect anymore?"

"No, not that," Michael frowned. "I mean that it's a good idea to go see MY brother Ralph. He's been so worried about you."

"Really? I mean, I don't even know your brother. I appreciate the concern, but..."

"So we'll just swing by the house and talk to Ralph," Boris continued. "He and Alice live there with your parents now, right?"

"Well yeah, but Ralph's at work, I think," Michael said, scratching his head.

"I thought he worked at Woody's?" Boris asked. "And Woody's is closed in case you didn't notice."

"Oh, I did," Michael said. "Ralph works at the stadium now, part-time. He cleans it by himself after every game."

"Whoa, intense!" Boris chuckled. "Isn't that like..."

"81,234 seats?" the driver said, suddenly depressed.

"Whoa, nice one, bro!" Boris laughed, reaching for a high-five before running his hand through his close-cropped hair. "I have no idea if you're right, but that SOUNDS good to me. Let's go there! I think they have a game tonight."

"I can't do that," the driver said, crossing his arms.

"What do you mean you CAN'T do that?!?" Boris said angrily. "You just asked us where we want to go and now you have to take us there. We're paying customers!"

"No we're not," Michael whispered far too loudly. "We don't have any money."

"DON'T HAVE ANY MONEY?!?!?!?" the driver shrieked, slamming his hands against the steering wheel. "FIRST, YOU HAVE THE NERVE TO ASK ME TO DRIVE TO THE STADIUM! THEN, YOU TELL ME YOU DON'T HAVE ANY MONEY! DO YOU THINK I WANT TO BE A CAB DRIVER? DO YOU? DO YOU?"

Ummm....

"What's wrong with the stadium?" Boris asked, trying to change the subject (unsuccessfully). "You're not a Nowhere Knights fan, are you?"

The cab driver gritted his teeth and started to shake. It looked like he was trying really hard not to say something. He did anyway, because, you know, these things happen.

Naturally.

"I'M DEQUAN 'HOT SHOT' ROBBINS!!!! DEQUAN 'HOT SHOT' ROBBINS!!!! DOESN'T THAT MEAN ANYTHING TO YOU?!? HUH? DOESN'T IT?!?"

"I'M BORIS FRANKFURTER!!!!!!! BORIS FRANKFURTER!!!!!!! I DON'T KNOW MY OWN MIDDLE NAME!!!" Boris yelled back.

"Wait a second," Michael said, shaking his head. "I know that name. You're ON the Some Town Fright! You were the guy who made fun of Razzmatazz at the Parade of Animals! You're dating that reporter, Cindy Wallace, right?"

"I was," Hot Shot nodded, closing his eyes.

He doesn't appear to be in the best football shape, Michael thought, looking him over.

Hot Shot may have been in the front seat, but Michael could tell that he looked more like Stan in a cabbie vest than any athlete he'd ever seen. Hot Shot's bulging stomach was bumping up against the steering wheel. He probably even used it to steer sometimes. How convenient.

"I got cut when that old grandpa Razzmatazz bought the team," Hot Shot said sadly. "I lost everything. My job. My wife. Cindy. It was a very dark, dark time."

"Are you out of it now so we can get a ride to the stadium?" Boris asked insensitively.

"I don't think I'll EVER get over it," Hot Shot sighed. "At least I got to be in the parade." He turned and stared out the window.

"Now what?" Michael asked. "I don't think we're getting a ride to the stadium."

"Of course we are, don't be crazy, man!" Boris said. "He just needs a minute."

A couple hours later, Michael looked up from a crossword puzzle and turned to Boris. "He hasn't moved. I think we should probably go. The game just ended."

Boris looked at Hot Shot. The football player was starting to drool on his shirt. He was fast asleep. "I hate to say it, but you're right. Let's do it," Boris nodded.

They got out of the cab and started to walk towards town. Michael turned around and threw something at the window. It hit the glass and fell to the ground.

"Wait...what WAS that?" Boris asked, confused.

"Money," Michael said, proud of his throw.

"I thought we didn't have any money?" Boris frowned, looking back at the cab.

"We didn't," Michael said. "But I found a box in the front seat with LOADS of cash in it. I just took some out and gave it back to him."

"That was his money," Boris said.

"Oh...." Michael trailed off. "Well...yeah, okay."

"Hey, so I think I know what Lord Piper's new invention is," Boris said.

"WHAT?" Michael gasped. "Why didn't you say anything earlier?"

"I don't know, I just like, thought about it," Boris said. "I didn't think it was important. I heard him mention something about a new necklace."

"A NEW necklace? What about the old ones?" Michael frowned.

"Apparently, they're starting to lose their power," Boris said. "At least I think. As Jerry develops more of the land and the forest is destroyed, its connection with the necklaces becomes weaker. Piper's plan is backfiring."

"Whoa, that's heavy," Michael said before shaking his head and scolding himself for using a ridiculous phrase like 'that's heavy.' "So what do the new necklaces do?"

"Not sure," Boris said. "But Lord Piper has a secret test subject to try them on. Either way, it can't be good."

"Yeah, not at all," Michael said. "Hey, we're here!"

He was right. It had only taken them five minutes to walk like five miles.

"How did that happen?!?!?" Boris wondered, looking around in surprise.

"No idea," Michael said. "But let's not question it. We have to find Ralph."

"Good idea."

They wandered through the maze of bonfires, misbehaving fans and general revelry and saw Ralph just inside the gate, scrubbing the entryway with a toothbrush. The team had won.

"I wonder if he's going to floss that too?" Michael laughed, waving to get his brother's attention. Ralph didn't see them so they started to scale the fence.

"Well, slap my fro! Is that YOU, Number One Fan?" a voice said behind them.

Michael turned around and jumped, falling to the ground. It was Razzmatazz! He was wearing a very cheap-looking, but probably expensive, green velvet suit.

"I know! Surprise! It's me! The league's NUMBER ONE owner!" Razzmatazz chuckled, putting his hand on Michael's shoulder. "How are you, BIG guy? Did you see the game?"

"Umm...not yet," Michael said.

"Not yet! The game's over!" Razzmatazz said, smiling. "Did you catch the game, Michael's clean-shaven friend?" he asked, turning to Boris.

"Yeah, bro! It was amazing!" Boris said going in for the high five.

*He has an honesty problem...*Michael thought.

"I KNEW IT!" Razzmatazz shouted, clapping his hands together.

Boris looked at his own hand awkwardly and put it in his pocket.

(No close cropped hair this time? No? Okay...)

"I bet you're wondering why I'm not in jail. You know, after the 'incident' at the parade," Razzmatazz said, making little quote signs with his fingers. "It's because I'm RICH! Filthy rich!" he laughed. "And when the team wouldn't let me play, I bought them! Take THAT Hot Shot!"

Michael frowned, remembering how upset the cab driver had been.

"Anyway, even thought it looks like you guys were trying to break into my stadium, I want to give you FREE TICKETS to the NEXT game! Owner's box, my treat!" Razzmatazz held out a stack of really large, expensive looking tickets. They were printed on gold leaf.

Maybe we can take the gold and give it to Hot Shot to pay for our cab ride? Michael thought. He shook his head. *Then again, he might not want tickets after all...*

"Now's the time to take the tickets!" Razzmatazz said through clinched teeth, smiling awkwardly.

Michael grabbed the tickets and put them in his fanny pack. *I can't believe I haven't put anything in here until now*, he frowned. *I hope I'm not growing out of fanny packs. They're SO handy!*

"Perfect! Well, off to the after party!" Razzmatazz laughed, adjusting his bow tie. "I think I'll call a cab. Maybe Hot Shot will pick me up?"

Fat chance...

"And he HAS too because I also own the cab company!" Razzmatazz said gleefully, pulling a stack of money out of his pocket and throwing it into the air. "I LOVE being rich!"

I bet...

"Goodbye, fans! I'll see you soon!" Razzmatazz skipped off, clutching his cell phone in his hand. Michael could hear Hot Shot screaming from miles away.

"Anyway, back to breaking in," Boris said, quickly scaling the fence.

Michael began to climb, but found that he was too scared to jump down when he got to the top. *Heights are worse from further up,* he thought.

Profound as always, Michael.

"Do you guys want me to open the gate for you?" Ralph asked, spotting them and walking over. He had an imprint on his face from where he'd fallen asleep cleaning.

"I don't think that would help at this point, Ralph," Michael said, looking down and closing his eyes.

"It's only like ten feet up so...you can probably just jump," Ralph said, shrugging.

"Yeah man, I'll catch you!" Boris said confidently.

Against his better judgment, Michael let go of the gate and crashed to the ground.

THUMP! THUMP! THUMP! THUMP! THUMP! THUMP! THUMP! THUMP! THUMP! (He rolled a bit...)

"HOLY CROW, YOU SAID YOU'D CATCH ME!!!" Michael yelled, glaring at Boris.

The bass player frowned, then smiled at Ralph. "It's good to see you, big guy!"

Ralph blinked then smiled back. "BORIS! I can't believe you're here! Wait until Alice and Margaret hear about this!"

SLAP!

Boris collapsed to the ground, clutching his face.

"I hope you don't mind, but I let myself in," Miss Dandelion said, lowering her hand to put her shoes back on (it's very difficult to hop a fence with heels). "Boris Frankfurter, you're in a LOT of trouble."

Boris lay on the ground, grabbing his face and screaming. He was so loud the entire parking lot turned to watch them. It was kind of embarrassing, really.

"It didn't actually hurt, did it?" Miss Dandelion gasped. She suddenly noticed the crowd watching them and became angry. "NOTHING TO SEE HERE!!!!" she yelled. "I didn't think I was that strong," she whispered.

"Nah," Boris laughed, sitting up. "I just wanted to give you a hard time. You actually missed."

What was the 'slap' sound then? Michael wondered.

Miss Dandelion scowled disapprovingly. "I don't think my sister would like it if you gave me a hard time."

"Probably not," Boris chuckled. "But I'm in the dog house anyway, so..."

"Her dog died last week," Miss Dandelion frowned.

"Oh...never liked that dog," Boris muttered, trailing off. "Wait, what's up with Ralph?" Michael's brother was laying on the ground, face down.

"CALL THE POLICE! CALL AN AMBULANCE! CALL SNEAKY PETE!" Michael yelled, panicking. Apparently, he had forgotten all about the pain he was supposed to be in from falling off the gate. I guess we can safely assume he's okay now?

"Oh my, did I hit him instead?!?" Miss Dandelion said, looking at her 'slapping' hand in surprise. She knelt down and checked Ralph's pulse. "He's alive, but barely."

"What the heck happened?!?" Michael asked, pushing Miss Dandelion out of the way so HE could check Ralph's pulse. "He's alive, but barely," he said, relieved.

"MY TURN!!!" Boris yelled excitedly. He was about to push Michael out of the way when Ralph woke up. "Whoa, bro! Where were you?" the bass player asked.

"We were SO worried!" Miss Dandelion cried, grabbing Ralph and pulling him in close.

"I think I just fell asleep," Ralph shrugged. "What's going on? Why are you guys freaking out and stuff?"

"I think I slapped you!" Miss Dandelion said. She pointed at Boris. "I REALLY meant to slap him!"

"But she didn't!!" Boris said, backing away.

"I'm sorry," Ralph said, standing up. "It's just that I've been so tired recently. After I lost my job at Woody's I looked everywhere. I only ended up here when the last guy died on the job. I don't have time to sleep. Or eat. Or do anything really. I'm glad you guys are here."

"Hey, speaking of being here," Miss Dandelion said angrily, turning to Boris. "WHERE IN THE WORLD HAVE YOU BEEN?"

"Please don't hit me," Boris said, attempting to cower behind Michael. Miss Dandelion lowered her hand.

"Well, if you won't think any less of me..." Boris began.

"Not possible," Miss Dandelion said.

"Good?" Boris frowned uncertainly. He launched into an epic tearful confession.

"Wait, so you're like not actually in a band?" Ralph asked, confused.

"That's all you got from that?!?!" Miss Dandelion said, disgusted. "Boris just confirmed that this Lord Piper guy is REAL. I mean, I remember a couple years ago when we met that talking hedgehog, but honestly, I'd kind of forgotten about it since then. It wasn't life changing."

*It was for me...*Michael thought.

"You've been lying to us the WHOLE time?" Ralph said, clearly hurt. He looked like he was going to pass out again, but Michael caught him. Ralph looked up, surprised.

"I'VE been working out!!!" Michael smiled triumphantly. "I have a lot of free time."

"So what you're saying is," Miss Dandelion said, folding her arms, "that even though things seem really GOOD in Some Town, that they're actually BAD?"

"Pretty much," Michael said. "Lord Piper has been using Jerry Mudwater to gain power around town. He has his eye on the mayor's seat next. Once he does that, he'll be in control of the whole city!"

"And he's developing a NEW line of necklaces," Boris added. "I can't imagine that the second one has an innocent purpose."

"BUT we have an advantage we didn't have last time," Michael said. "After I escaped from Mom and Dad's, we met up with the Sleeve. Apparently, they've been in touch with someone on the inside."

"Who is it?" Ralph asked, scratching his head. "This is a lot to take in. Especially since I stopped believing in this stuff."

"We're not sure," Michael shrugged. "But that's not all. The contact believes he knows where the three-legged cat and the angry turtle are keeping Crispin and Wiggly Tom."

"Wait, who's the three-legged cat?" Miss Dandelion asked.

Okay, STOP! STOP! STOP! STOP! STOP! As your narrator, I feel that it's important to pause the story here and give Ralph and Miss Dandelion some time to catch up. After all, it's only polite, and I've been told that I am quite the gentleman. It's been two years and a lot has been going on. Lord Piper's evil plans, the cat's evil plans, the Sleeve's turmoil, Grandpa Pumpernickel's jailing, Michael's imprisonment, Boris' rap career- the list goes on. I'm sure YOU need a minute to digest it all as well. It's heavy stuff, and it shouldn't be taken lightly. Lives are in danger, and the future of Some Town is at stake...

...Well, how do you feel now? Okay, you need another minute...Hey, take your time....

...Okay, really now. We have to get started!

"Man, that's a LOT going on," Ralph said, taking a deep breath. "I had no idea we were in so much danger!"

Michael thought he didn't sound convinced.

"Yeah, and it's probably even worse than we think, bro!" Boris said. "But the good thing is, Cephas was able to figure out the address of where the cat might be. Here it is, take a look."

"Wait, really?" Ralph said, laughing. "I know EXACTLY where this is!"

"You do?!?" Michael asked, confused. "Are you up to no good? Have you turned to drugs? I'm going to tell Mom and Dad!"

Ralph shook his head. "No, Michael. I'M going to tell Mom and Dad you escaped from school again. Trust me, they won't be happy."

No, no they won't...

"Just kidding," Ralph said, winking. "I'm coming. I don't want to go home either. Then I'd have to admit that I saw you and didn't bring you with me."

"So you're covering your OWN back?" Michael asked.

"Partly, but Mom and Dad probably aren't home anyway. They were out looking for you the last time I checked. Also, I know this is important. I didn't believe it before, but it's hard not to after everything you've told me. Plus, I can show you around."

"Well, if you're going, I'm going too," Miss Dandelion said.

"No way," Ralph frowned, shaking his head. "It's too dangerous."

"Then why do I get to go?" Michael asked. "I'm only eleven."

"Actually, you're thirteen," Ralph said, surprised he remembered.

Oh yeah. Golly, how time flies!

"I'm going and that's final!" Miss Dandelion said in a tone that Ralph recognized all too well. There was no arguing with her. "Let me at least text my sister and let her know where we are so she doesn't get worried. Now that you're back, Boris, she can come home."

"NO!" Boris yelled. Embarrassed, he looked around, thinking he'd attracted the crowd's attention again. No such luck. Or, not luck. They were all gone!

How long have we been talking?!?! Michael wondered. *And why haven't I eaten anything recently?!?!?* He looked down and saw a kernel of popcorn on the ground. *Aha! Ralph missed a spot.* He reached down and popped it into his mouth. *They're better cooked, but the crunchiness is kind of exciting.*

"I mean, please don't!" Boris said, frowning. "I don't want her to be in danger too."

"Fine," Miss Dandelion said, putting her phone behind her back and texting her sister anyway.

(Naturally, what else would you expect?)

"Then it's settled, let's go!" Ralph said, putting his cleaning supplies away and locking the gate behind them.

*I don't want to go. I don't like danger...*Michael frowned. But he DID want to see Crispin, and if this was the only way he could do that, he was in.

"I'm IN!" he said, as they piled into Ralph's new, but actually old, second-hand truck. Boris sat in the back.

"That was never in question, Michael," Ralph said, taking one last look at the stadium as they pulled away.

"Oh," Michael said. "So where are we going?"

"The last place I thought I'd have to go tonight," Ralph said. "The Some Town Fright storage warehouse."

"So wait, the TEAM owns this place?" Michael asked, as they pulled up to an abandoned-looking warehouse. "It's kind of shabby."

It also needs redecorating...

"Razzmatazz figures no one will steal anything if it looks like this," Ralph shrugged.

"But doesn't that actually increase the probability? You know, because it seems empty?" Miss Dandelion asked, checking her phone for a reply from her sister.

"I guess so," Ralph laughed. "And either way, WE'RE visiting it."

"But we're not technically breaking in because you work here, bro," Boris said.

"But I don't have my key, so we ARE breaking in," Ralph said, shaking his head.

They walked around, looking for a way in. When they couldn't find one, Boris started to pick the lock with a rusty nail he found on the ground.

"I learned how to do this when I was on tour with the Lobsters," he said. "Our manager got locked in the bathroom, and I had to break him out between songs."

"You didn't do that, you're not in a band," Miss Dandelion said, scowling. She pushed Boris to the side and kicked at the door. It came splintering to the ground. "There, that's better."

Ralph's mouth hung open.

"What?" she asked. "I've been working out..."

Me too! I could have done that? Michael thought.

As they walked inside, it took Michael's eyes a few seconds to adjust. The place was a mess! Aisles and aisles of memorabilia stretched before them wall-to-wall.

"Yeah, I was supposed to organize this," Ralph said. "But no one goes here but me, and I know where everything is."

Makes sense.

"Have you seen any sign of Crispin or the three-legged cat?" Michael asked hopefully.

"Nah, sorry man," Ralph said.

The warehouse was quiet, and according to Ralph, everything seemed to be in place.

"Let's split up," Boris suggested. "That way we can cover more ground."

"That's not a good idea at all!" Michael said, his eyes wide. "That's usually when people DIE! I don't want to die! I want to eat!"

"We have a crate of Rainbow Chips in the back if you want to check there first," Ralph laughed. "Boris is right though. If we're going to find Crispin and the others, we have to separate. I have to be at work in the morning."

"You're already here!" Michael said, hoping that somehow his comments would help keep them together.

"I have to be at the stadium," Ralph said.

Michael frowned as they all started to walk in opposite directions. A chill ran up his spine. *This isn't a good idea,* he thought. *This isn't a good idea at ALL...*

He'd seen a LOT of movies about creepy warehouses and something bad always happened. He was thankful he wasn't in a movie, but he wasn't so sure bad stuff didn't happen to people in books too. If so, he was in a book. Suddenly, a terrifying sound broke the silence!

BANG! BANG! BANG! BANG!

I knew it! Oh junk, I just KNEW IT!!!! Michael thought, his heart racing. He looked around, trying to find somewhere to hide. A Razzmatazz bobblehead smiled at him from a pile of boxes in the corner.

This is the worst, he thought, diving to the ground.

"SORRY GUYS, IT WAS JUST MY CELL PHONE!" Boris yelled from the other side of the warehouse. "IT WAS A REMINDER TO TELL ME THAT IT'S A BAD IDEA TO SPLIT UP INTO GROUPS! HEY...WAIT A SECOND...WHO ARE YOU?!?!? AHHHHHHHH!!!!!!!"

"BORIS?!?!?!? ARE YOU OKAY?!?!?!? WHAT HAPPENED?!?!?!? Ralph yelled.

Michael could hear him walking toward where Boris had disappeared.

"Ralph! Get away from there," Miss Dandelion whispered. "It's going to get you too."

"What is?" Ralph asked. "Wait...AHHHHHHH!!!!"

"RALPH!" Miss Dandelion screamed. "AHHHH!"

The warehouse was silent. Michael knew that whatever had taken Boris, Ralph and Miss Dandelion was after him next. He tried to crawl deeper into the pile, but accidently knocked over a box full of bobbleheads in the process. It came crashing down on him.

Michael's heart froze. Had they heard him?!?! Had IT heard him?!?! Why had he hidden in a pile of bobbleheads instead of a bunch of Rainbow Chips?!?!?

Then suddenly, without warning, everything went black.

When Michael woke up, he found that he was chained to a table. *Great. I've been getting chained to a LOT of stuff recently. This is entirely not ideal.*

Sighing, he looked down and gasped. The table was filthy! *Good thing I'm up to date on my shots,* he thought.

As he glanced around the room, he decided he must be in a cavern underneath the warehouse. *This seems like an unnecessary place for a football team to have.* The room smelled damp, like the air was old and wet. *Gross...*

Suddenly, a bright light shone down on him.

"GAHHHHHHHHHHHHHHHHH!!!!!" he yelled.

"It's about time you woke up," a voice said. Wait a second...Michael recognized that voice!

"The three-legged cat!" he said, horrified. *I KNEW it! Or...I was hoping that's who it was since we were looking for him. But I didn't want to meet THIS way. I wanted HIM to be on the table. Which, you know, sounds kind of weird.*

"I DO have a name, you know," the cat said darkly.

"Whatever," Michael said.

"You were always such an insolent little boy," the cat snapped, placing something sharp on the table beside Michael's head.

"Well, thank you!" Michael said, smiling. Nobody had ever called him insolent before! Which is probably why he didn't know that it meant 'rude, or arrogant.'

"I wouldn't be laughing if I were you," the cat said.

Michael heard a sharpening sound somewhere in the room. A door opened behind him.

"Ah, my assistant is here!" the cat said. "Michael, I would like you to meet the Cardinal cardinal. He's one of the chief elders of Dexterum Dei."

The cardinal came into view and sneered. He was wearing a red medical gown and a surgical mask. That couldn't be a good thing! Then again, nothing about

Michael's current situation was really all that fantastic so what did it matter?

"You must be confused," the cat said, placing a gag in Michael's mouth. "I was too before I was enlightened. You see, my friends and I used to be part of a monastery, Three Paws Hall. Have you heard of it?"

Michael tried to scream.

"No matter," the cat continued. "Life was good for a while. We would spend all day worshipping God in order to grow closer to Him. It was everything I had ever wanted. But one day I realized I didn't actually want to know God, I wanted to BE God. I wanted power! I couldn't believe what I had been missing out on this whole time!"

Yeah, no kidding...

"I'm sure right now you're thinking that I'm a horrible person," the cat said as he began to fill an extremely long syringe. "But that's where you're wrong! I had dedicated my entire life to God, and how did He repay me? With an orphan on our doorstep! Did we ask for that? NO! Our resources were stretched thin already."

The Cardinal cardinal nodded in agreement.

"Yet, for a while, everything was fine," the cat said. "Then, the boy grew up and started to cause trouble. He was rebellious! He too was insolent! And so the time came when we were forced to kick him out! We had no choice!"

Lord Piper? Michael frowned. *So THIS is the abbot Grandpa was talking about?!?! THIS is the man....errr...cat, that turned Lord Piper into a monster?!?*

"You may think we're heartless, but it's what we HAD to do," the cat continued. "The boy had no interest in the things of God. We were a monastery, God was our job! It wasn't until later we realized our mistake. God must have had no hand in this! So we formed Dexterum Dei, the Right Hand of God, to carry out His work on Earth. To use our power for His purposes. And that's why we find ourselves here beneath this warehouse today. To conduct experiments that will defeat Lord Piper forever! It is God's will."

The cat threw back his head to laugh. He nudged the cardinal, and the bird joined in. The terrible sound of their happiness echoed around the cavern.

Michael shuddered beneath the chains. He hoped that wherever his friends were, they were safe. *Maybe they didn't get captured by the same people?* he wondered.

"Woo, that was fun," the cat said, wiping the tears out of his eyes and gasping for air. "It's not often we get to have this much fun!"

"You got that right, boss," the cardinal said, handing the cat a filthy looking handkerchief. "Except on karaoke night. That's hard to beat!"

"But, all good things must come to an end," the cat said, testing the syringe. A thick green liquid squirted out of the top. "Or begin, depending on how you look at it," he chuckled. "Michael, this is my own special formula. It has been used exactly once. Once you are injected, you will become the ultimate weapon against Lord Piper! At least that's what we think will happen."

What does that even mean?

"And perhaps, you will not suffer the same painful death as Subject One. What a strange and uncooperative character. What was he again? A deer?"

The cardinal nodded.

Wiggly Tom? Michael gasped. He started to choke, coughing and heaving on the table. The cardinal removed the gag and Michael breathed in deeply.

"Don't get too excited," the cat said, his eyes flashing with danger. "My associate and I only want to hear you scream when the transformation begins!"

As the syringe began to close in on Michael's arm, he started to think about everyone he loved. Ralph and Miss Dandelion. The villagers. The Sleeve. Maybe Boris. Possibly Lucy, although he was still undecided about her. His parents. Crispin...

Suddenly, a terrifying scream rang out from somewhere in the basement. The angry turtle burst into the room, a furious look on his face. "It's the girl!" he snapped. "She won't stop screaming! She believes the boy is dead."

"Good," the cat said, looking at the syringe and placing it down on the table. "Our evil plan worked! Bring in one of the others." He stood over Michael and began to laugh. "Today is your lucky day, boy. With you 'dead,' it means that I can continue my tests without any problem. It's over. Especially for your girlfriend..."

Michael tried to scream, but the cardinal had stuffed the gag back in his mouth.

A few moments earlier...You know, before the scream and all that. Ralph woke up screaming himself. "WAIT! STOP! GO AWAY!!!!" he yelled. He didn't want to be captured.

As his eyes adjusted to his surroundings, he saw that he was in a large cage underground, probably beneath the warehouse. He was sort-of relieved to see that Boris and Miss Dandelion were with him, but they were still out cold. Michael was nowhere to be found.

"Figures HE didn't get captured," Ralph muttered.

"Are you Michael's brother?" a voice asked.

Ralph turned around and saw a small girl sitting in the corner. She looked to be about Michael's age and had long, brown hair. Her clothes were filthy like she had been here for a while. Which, honestly, she probably had. Ralph's options for escaping weren't too good right now.

"Unfortunately," he laughed.

The girl smiled. "I'm Crispin! Crispin Elizabeth Rye. I'm in Michael's class. Or, I was..."

"Wait a second," Ralph said. "Rye...Rye...your Dad owns Hungry Woody's, right? I used to work there!"

"That's him! Is he okay?" Crispin asked, a look of concern on her face.

"I'm not sure," Ralph said. "If what Michael says is true, then your dad is in trouble."

"What?!?" Crispin gasped. "What do you mean?"

"Well, Michael told me that Lord Piper is trying to ruin the lives of the monks from his old monastery. Is your dad connected to that somehow? Woody's closed down months ago and no one has heard from him since then. He used to talk about you all the time. I..." Ralph said, choosing his words carefully. "I'm so sorry, I don't know what to say."

"I don't know anything anymore," Crispin shrugged, starting to cry.

*Ah crap...*Ralph thought.

"HEY, WHY DON'T YOU TWO CAN IT BEFORE I BASH YOUR HEADS IN!" a voice screamed from down the hallway. The noise woke up the others.

"Hey, what's going on, guys?" Boris asked, sitting up and stretching. When one of his hands hit the side of the cell, he shrieked and opened his eyes. "GUYS! What IS this place?!"

"I said...CAN IT!" the voice yelled, closer this time.

"We're in the basement of the warehouse," Ralph said. "This is Crispin, Michael's friend."

"Girlfriend, actually," Crispin smiled weakly.

"Wait, what?!?!" Ralph asked, confused. "Anyway," he said, shaking his head. "Her dad used to own Hungry Woody's. Or, I mean, he still does if he's not dead."

"RALPH!" Miss Dandelion said, frowning. "That's not a very sensitive thing to say."

"It's okay, it's true," Crispin sobbed.

"Wait, guys, there's a BEAR IN HERE!!!!!!" Boris yelled, jumping up and rushing to the side of the cage. "Let me out of here, bro!"

"Oh, that's just Ruxiben," Crispin laughed. "He's hibernating."

The peddler lay in the far corner of the cell, fast asleep and eating his hat. Moe had been wrong. Ruxiben wasn't at the Sleeve at all. He'd been captured! Or, he had come down here voluntarily, which wasn't as likely. Then again, it wasn't an AWFUL spot to get some shut eye.

"That was mad scary," the bass player said, turning around and staring at the bear uneasily.

BANG! BANG! BANG! BANG! BANG!

"WHOA!" Boris yelled, jumping behind Ralph.

"I told you losers to chill the HECK OUT," a man growled, glaring at them through the bars. It was Josh, the camera guy from News Channel 90613. What an unexpected turn!

"Hey, aren't you on TV?" Ralph asked. He'd been forced to watch the news with his mom one time.

It had scarred him for life.

"Yeah, what about it?" Josh asked, raising his camera and pressing the 'record' button. "Razzmatazz asked me to come here to report on the progress of the serum. He doesn't trust those animals. I wouldn't either, but at least they helped him out. That's what matters."

"What do you mean?" Miss Dandelion asked.

"It wasn't Razzmatazz's money that got him out of jail," Crispin said, glaring at the cameraman. "It was the cat. He needed somewhere to hide while he was conducting his experiments so they decided to work together."

"So wait," Boris said, scratching his head. "There's a cat working with your boss, Ralph?"

"I guess so," Ralph said, trying to put the pieces together. He hated cats. This only confirmed his feelings. "But don't blame me, I didn't know."

"No one knows," Josh laughed. "That's the beauty of it. Razzmatazz can continue his job with the news station, while being the beloved owner of Some Town's favorite team. No one will ever suspect he's working with a secret organization, providing funds for inhumane experiments and plotting his own violent and greedy takeover of the town. It's just perfect!"

"That's SO devious!" Boris said, amazed.

"It's EVIL!" Crispin said angrily, walking over to Josh and spitting in his face.

Josh chuckled. "But that's not the worst of it!" he said. "There's a reason you're all here. Razzmatazz agreed to be on the lookout for Michael. When he overheard you were going to his warehouse, well, it was too good to be true. But it wasn't. HAHAHAHAHAHAHA!"

"THAT TRAITOR!!!" Ralph shouted, knocking the camera out of Josh's hands and grabbing him by the neck.

"ENOUGH!" a voice yelled. It was the angry turtle. "It doesn't matter. It's over."

"What do you mean, it's over?" Crispin asked, afraid of what she might hear.

The turtle stared at them with a triumphant grin. "Michael Pumpernickel is dead!"

Crispin began to scream as the turtle and Josh laughed maniacally, holding hands and smiling. Miss Dandelion collapsed into Ralph's arms, too overwhelmed to say anything. Even Boris began to cry. As their sorrows echoed through the walls and into the next room, Michael Pumpernickel, very much still alive, tried to scream.

Michael was ready to give up. No matter how hard he tried, he couldn't get Crispin's screams out of his head. He wanted to tell the cat to inject him and leave the others alone, but the gag was still in his mouth. Super bad luck.

The cardinal and turtle had disappeared, and the cat was humming to himself as he laid out an arrangement of swords, knives, axes and other things that had no place in an operating room.

"This day is turning out to be even BETTER than I thought!" the cat said brightly. "You see, it all started when I found a Sneaky Pete toy in my breakfast cereal. THAT was unexpected! Do you like Sneaky Pete, Michael?"

Michael nodded. *Well yeah, but it sickens me that YOU like him too...*

"I thought so, most people do," the cat chuckled. "I like him because he's a hero. Why, I have all of his books in the next room! He always does what needs to be done for the greater good. Not everyone is willing to do that. I'm like Sneaky Pete, don't you think?"

Again Michael nodded before catching himself and trying to un-nod. The cat frowned.

"Ah, no matter," he continued. "Your opinion is of little consequence. Some of the greatest minds were ridiculed in their day! Why, did you know that the creator of Distant Galaxy was imprisoned three years for going 110mph in a 45mph zone? Didn't they know he was in hyper drive?"

Even hyper drive has speed limits! Everyone knows that. What kind of uncivilized world does he live in?

"And the guy who created Wild Animals in the Wild got picked on for wearing animal skins to school. Did he let that stop him? No! Absolutely not! He pushed ahead. That's what I'M doing here, Michael. Someone has to."

"FDHGSO DOSID DS SDGHISDO AJD DOISD!" Michael tried to yell.

"I'm not sure I know what you mean," the cat said, gazing at an especially long knife.

"FDHGSO DOSID DS SDGHISDO AJD DOISD!"

"If you're asking me to take the gag out of your mouth, I'm afraid I can't," the cat said, shaking his head. "Then your little friends might know you're still alive. Where's the fun in THAT?!?"

They sat in silence.

"Ah, why not," the cat laughed, pulling the gag out of Michael's mouth. "Everything is going my way today, anyway! What was it that you said earlier?"

"Umm...I'm really not sure. Sorry," Michael said truthfully. Except maybe the 'sorry' part...

"WHAT DO YOU MEAN NOT SURE?!?!?!" the cat snapped, holding the knife up to Michael's face. "I waited all that time for NOTHING!!!!"

"It's not my fault," Michael said. "I didn't want the gag in there anyway."

"You INFURIATE me!" the cat said angrily, slamming his paws down on the table.

Suddenly, the cardinal reentered the room, followed by an enormous man in chains.

"BROSKI! YOU'RE ALIVE!!!" Boris said happily.

"STOP. NO," the cat said, glaring at Michael and waving his hand. "I know you were about to say something annoying, so I just wanted to put a stop to it before it happened." He stuffed the gag back into Michael's mouth.

That's not fair...I hadn't even decided what I was going to say yet! Usually I just start talking to see what comes out!

"Let's make this quick, boss, the prisoners are getting restless," the cardinal said, looking nervous. "We don't want any 'accidents.'"

"That's precisely what we DO want!" the cat said, putting the knife down and grabbing the green-filled syringe. "When they're restless, they're desperate. And when they're desperate, they're willing to do anything. Right, surprisingly well-kept man?" He looked Boris up and down.

"I don't really have a choice, do I?" Boris asked, his eyes wide with panic. "Because if I do, I'd rather bow out now. That looks sharp." He glanced nervously at Michael.

"Oh, it's VERY sharp," the cat chuckled.

"Very sharp," the cardinal echoed, winking.

"So you'd rather I inject Michael?" the cat asked, placing the syringe at Michael's neck.

"NO! DON'T! HE'S GOT SO MUCH TO LIVE FOR! HE'S ONLY ELEVEN!" Boris yelled.

I'm actually, thirteen. Ralph reminded me of that.

"And what do YOU have to live for?" the cat asked, moving the needle back to Boris. He was really enjoying the suspense. Michael guessed he had probably been practicing this moment for years on all sorts of stuffed animals and action figures.

And Wiggly Tom.

"Well, there's my band..." Boris said, realizing he couldn't think very well without scratching his close cropped hair. "Oh wait, that's not true, I'm not in a band..."

"HAHA, you see, Cardinal? No one will miss him!" the cat laughed triumphantly. "What do you think, Michael? Do you agree?"

Michael struggled with his restraints. There was nothing he could do!

"I guess I'll take that as a 'yes,'" the cat shrugged, driving the needle through Boris' skin.

As the serum emptied into the bass player's arm, he screamed and started to shake violently on the table. He turned toward Michael, growling, foam coming out of his mouth. The cat and cardinal watched curiously, as Boris' eyes turned green and the chains began to crumble. Just before he broke free, the convulsions suddenly stopped, and the bass player collapsed on the table.

The cardinal walked over and checked Boris' pulse.

"Nothing," he said, shaking his head.

"Well, did it work?" the turtle asked, coming into the room.

"NO," the cat snapped, kicking the table and knocking Boris to the floor. "It was just like last time with the deer. Go get Josh and make him clean up this mess!"

The turtle looked at Boris' body and shook his head.

"NOW!!!!!!" the cat screamed.

Not wanting to be left alone with the cat, the cardinal quickly followed him through the door.

"Do you know how long I've waited for this moment, Michael?" the cat sighed, leaning against the operating table. "Decades! You see, as the abbot of the monastery, it was MY job to promote order. I failed in that respect. We never should have allowed Lord Piper into our midst. He's a monster! Since then, everything I've done has been to make that wrong right. It's my life's work."

Michael thought back to the conversation he had with Lord Piper at the parade and began to wonder who the bad guy REALLY was. Lord Piper was just fighting back, wasn't he? Isn't that what Michael was doing? What made him any different?

"I got the BEST footage of when the turtle told them he was dead!" Josh laughed, holding up the camera as he entered the room. Not impressed, the turtle pushed it aside and helped the cardinal bring in another subject.

IT WAS RALPH!!!!

Oh gosh! Michael thought. *I need to think of something quick! And being quick isn't one of my strong points. Making LISTS of my strong points is one of my strong points! I wonder if that can help me here? Probably not because I can't feel my hands...*

Just like Boris, they chained Ralph to one of the tables and put a gag in his mouth. Ralph looked over at his brother, too shocked to speak. He had been crying.

"Take that one out of here," the cat said to Josh, pointing at Boris' body.

"Why can't I ever do the cool stuff?!?!" Josh asked angrily, putting the video camera in his pocket. "I don't think you guys truly appreciate how great of a videographer I am. At least Razzmatazz recognizes my genius."

Are you kidding?!?! Michael thought. *He hates you!*

"We don't care," the cat said. "NOW SCRAM!!!!!"

...which is an ironic thing for a cat to say since that's something people usually say TO cats. You know?

Josh frowned and began to drag Boris out of the room.

"Now, Michael," the cat said, removing the gag again. "Do you have any last words for your brother?"

Michael didn't know WHAT to say. The whole time, throughout this crazy adventure, his own life had been in danger. Sure, he'd lost some people along the way, but he'd always counted on his family being safe. That much he knew. But now Ralph lay where Boris had moments before. At the time, Michael had been filled with anger. Now he was defeated.

"Ralph, it's going to be okay," he whispered. He didn't even believe it himself.

"Is that IT?!?!" the cat laughed, taking a syringe from the cardinal. This time, it contained a deep purple liquid. "You used to be SUCH a chatterbox! I bet your parents wish they'd tried this earlier!"

He shook his head, placing the gag back in Michael's mouth. "And what about you?" he asked, walking over to Ralph. "Give me something, please! You're both so boring now it's giving me a headache!"

Michael's brother closed his eyes and sighed like he was going to say something difficult. "I believe you, Michael," Ralph said finally.

Michael looked at him, confused.

"I believe everything," Ralph said. "About Lord Piper, and your friends and the necklaces. I know it's pretty stupid to say that now after all we've been through."

"It really is," the cardinal interrupted.

"Stop talking, you FOOL! I want to hear the rest of this. It's wonderful!" the cat said gleefully. He was taking a picture of himself in the operating room.

"I also wanted to let you know something else," Ralph said. "I've been working with the Nervous Sleeve for the past two years."

WHAT?!?!?! Michael thought.

"Oh, this is GOOD!" the cat said, clapping his paws together.

"I know I should have told you sooner, but I had no way of contacting them," Ralph frowned. "They contacted ME. I got the first letter a month after you came home. It talked about all the same things you'd been telling me for WEEKS! It was incredible! We've been looking for this place ever since then. We've been looking for Crispin too. I just....I just wanted you to know."

Ralph trailed off as Michael's tears began to fill with tears (if that's possible). He didn't know what to think. He didn't know what to say. His brother, Ralph, had been working with the Sleeve all along! Michael wanted to save him. He wanted to give him a hug! But there was nothing he could do.

The cat cleared his throat, dabbing at his eyes. "Thank you, Ralph, that was beautiful."

"Are you crying?" Ralph scowled. "Seriously?"

"Of course not!" the cat snapped, quickly turning away from them. "What was I saying? You've made me forget what I was saying!"

"I don't know," Ralph said.

The cat shrieked and dropped the syringe. "We don't have time for this nonsense!" he said, fumbling the needle as he picked it up. "I DON'T EVEN KNOW WHY I BOTHER ANYMORE!"

"WAIT!" Ralph said, looking panicked. "I can help! I have leverage against Lord Piper! We can stop him together!"

Michael blinked. *What's going on?!?*

"I'm sure we could," the cat said, shaking his head. "But this is MY fight! We all have a part to play." He plunged the needle into Ralph's skin!

"NOOOOOOOOO!!!!" Michael yelled.

Ralph's eyes rolled to the back of his head. Unlike Boris, he lay still on the table.

"Go check him!" the cat snapped, motioning to the cardinal. "This is a brand new formula, completely different from the first one!"

The cardinal walked over hesitantly and put his ear to Ralph's chest. "You're not going to like this, boss..."

"Wait..." the turtle said. "What's that sound?"

BOOM. BOOOM. BOOOMMM. BOOOOOMMM.

"It sounds like it's coming from upstairs," the cat said, looking for someone to blame. "Which one of you two was up there last?"

The cardinal and turtle both pointed at each other.

BOOM. BOOOM. BOOOMMM. BOOOOOMMM.

"It wasn't me, boss, I promise!" the cardinal said. "Josh is probably just tap dancing again."

Suddenly, the door crashed to the ground!

Everything happened so quickly, Michael could barely keep up! *GRUMPY OLD MS. JONES?* he gasped, as she ran over and ripped the chains from the table.

"I needed that!" she said, nodding to him as she dove back into the fray.

Now free, he sat up and surveyed the scene around him. Members of the Nervous Sleeve were attacking the room with foam fingers, roasted peanuts and an assortment of merchandise from upstairs. He chuckled.

"I HOPE WE'RE NOT TOO LATE!!!" Moe yelled, smiling at Michael as he attacked the turtle with a stack of baseball cards.

Sensing that the tides were turning, the cat desperately injected Ralph with five more syringes. "YOU'RE TOO LATE!" he cackled, raising each syringe for dramatic effect. "My plan worked perfectly! I've created a monster!" he laughed, looking down at Ralph and stroking his head.

"NO ONE STROKES MY BROTHER!" Michael screamed, falling down and hitting his head on the side of the table.

"Michael, are you okay?" Mable asked, kneeling down beside him. "We have to go! Schumer is out of peanuts and Moe thinks Stan is hiding in the car."

Michael blinked. "Crispin is that you?" he asked, staring at the mole blankly. "Tell your dad I DON'T want another triple pickle, mutton glutton, big time burger. It hurts my head."

Mable frowned, propping him up against the wall. "There you go, dear," she said, ducking as a souvenir football flew past them. "You're just not right."

"I'M okay," Michael said, slurring his words. "I just had too much three spice cider. That stuff really packs a PUNCH if you know what I mean." He began to laugh uncontrollably.

"And here we were worried about Ralph," Mable muttered. "Go figure."

"When you SHOULD be worried about ME!"

Mable spun around and saw that the turtle was standing over her with a really long knife.

"What did you do with Moe?!?!" she asked angrily, looking around for something to defend herself with.

"I'm right here!" Moe said. He was desperately trying to break Ralph's chains with a foam noodle. "I thought I'd put that guy down!"

"Not for long!" the turtle said, pulling a Razzmatazz Rookie Card out of a brutal cut on his leg. "Now it's YOUR turn to suffer."

"You mean like do math homework?" Michael asked, confused.

"What is he talking about?" the turtle snapped, glaring at them with distaste. "Make him stop talking."

"YOU FIRST!" Mable yelled, grabbing a seat cushion off the floor and pointing it at his head.

The turtle chuckled, dropping his knife to the ground. "I guess you've got me. You win." He raised his hands in defeat.

"I can't believe it! I've never won anything before!" Michael mumbled, drifting in and out of sleep. Drool began to run down his face.

"Then today's your lucky day!" the turtle yelled, pulling an unused syringe out of his shell.

Mable gasped.

"But I think you already knew that because my associate told you earlier! At least, I THINK he did!" the turtle frowned, charging toward them.

WHAM! WHAM! WHAM! WHAM! WHAM!

The sound woke Michael up, bringing him out of his stupor. The turtle lay on the ground, knocked out. The syringe, still unused, lay next to him. Confused, Michael looked up and saw Moe standing with a foam noodle.

"These things are awful on chains, but they do a pretty good job on turtles," he laughed. "Just something to keep in mind." He held out his hand to help Michael up.

"Thanks," Michael said. "I don't know what to say!"

"Save your breath, we have to get out of here," Moe said, looking around nervously. The whole room began to shake, as chunks of the ceiling began to fall on them. "We must have caused some sort of structural damage when we blasted through the door! The whole thing's coming down! Can I count on you to stay with me?"

Michael nodded.

"Good," Moe said. "Grab the turtle. Margaret can get the cat. I'll get Ralph. Does anybody know where the others are?"

"I think they're back there," Michael said, pointing to a door at the far end of the room. He could barely see it over all of the smoke.

"It's not going to be easy, but we have to try," Moe frowned, a look of determination on his face.

A light fixture crashed to the ground, nearly hitting Mable in the head. "Well, are we just going to stand here and get our goose cooked?" she asked.

"No, Mable, we have to be quick. Really quick!"

"THEN LET'S GO!" Mable yelled.

Now, just like Moe said, it only seems appropriate that this part of the story would be quick. After all, if I gave you a long, drawn-out explanation, it would seem like Michael and the Sleeve were in even greater danger than before! Let's not do that. I know you're worried, so let's just go ahead and skip to the good part. You know, where they're already back safe and sound at the Nervous Sleeve.

"Wow, that WAS quick!" Michael said, glancing around. He was back in the kitchen of Hungry Woody's with the others. "What happened?"

"You saved us, THAT'S what happened," Miss Dandelion said gratefully.

"I did?" Michael asked, confused.

"You were a hero, Michael," Moe said. "We couldn't have done it without you."

"But I don't remember anything," Michael said, scratching his head.

"Really?" Cephas asked. "You're not tired? I've never seen someone move so quickly!"

Everyone nodded in agreement.

What a curious day, Michael thought. "Hey, wait, Cephas, I didn't even see you there!"

165

"Are you kidding?" Ms. Jones asked. "Cephas spotted the cage!"

"He's blind! How did he do that?" Michael frowned.

"I wouldn't worry about it," Moe chuckled, waving his hand dismissively. "The point is you're all here, safe and sound. Ralph is fine. The cat and turtle are gone. We even have animals out looking for Boris and Josh! Everything's taken care of."

"But...but..." Michael said. "Ralph, you got injected by all that stuff!"

"Yeah, I guess it cancelled itself out, I don't know," Ralph shrugged.

Michael wasn't convinced. "What if the cat and turtle come after us?"

"They won't, Michael," Mable said as she stirred a fresh pot of soup. "They didn't make it out before the building collapsed."

"Oh," Michael said. "But what about the cardinal?"

"Cardinal?" Cephas said, confused. "We didn't see a cardinal..."

Of course YOU didn't...

"And what about Boris? How do we know he's okay?" Michael said frantically.

Grumpy Old Ms. Jones started to cry.

Ah, crap...

"Michael, Michael, it's fine! It's fine," Moe said, walking over and putting an arm around him. "And anyway, don't you have more important things to worry about?" He pointed across the room to the most beautiful girl Michael had ever seen.

Crispin! Michael thought, running across the room and knocking her over.

"Hey, Michael!" Crispin said brightly. She looked a lot better than she had the day before. Not that she ever looked 'BAD' bad. But you know.

"I guess you're not dead AFTER all," she said, smiling. It was the most amazing thing he'd ever seen. Just thinking about it had gotten him through the toughest moments of the past two years. Her beautiful lips...

STOP. Too mushy.

"So wait..." Michael said, holding hands with Crispin. "How did you guys know where to find us?"

"Oh, it was easy," Ms. Jones said, wiping the tears from her eyes. "Alice texted me!"

"But I thought..."

"Don't say his name," Miss Dandelion mouthed.

"I thought that...umm...umm..." Michael began, forgetting what he was talking about. *This happens to me at an alarming rate...*

"I texted her anyway because that's what sisters do!" Miss Dandelion smiled.

"Right. And when I couldn't get in touch with Alice or Ralph when I got back into town," Ms. Jones said, "I contacted Moe. I didn't know he was supposed to be dead. No offense."

"None taken," Moe said. "I much prefer this to being dead." (Don't we all?)

"He was concerned about you guys too, so we went to the address on the piece of paper. That's when we, well...you know the rest."

I don't really. I've been trying to figure out what happened for a while now!

"HEY GUYS!!!!!" Schumer said, suddenly.

Michael jumped. He hadn't seen him come in.

"We just got another letter from our contact with Lord Piper! He wants us to meet him at the Some Town Fright game tomorrow! Or, um..." he said, glancing at his watch (he has a watch!?!). "Actually, later today!"

"I was invited to that game!" Michael said, remembering the tickets in his fanny pack.

"Perfect!" Moe said. "The contact would probably want to meet you anyway. I think it's best if someone else goes with too. Safety in numbers!"

"If only Omar was here, he'd be SO excited," Stan said sadly, pulling down his sweater vest to cover his bulging stomach.

"I'll go," Ralph said firmly.

"But Ralph, dear! You're still recovering!" Miss Dandelion said, a look of concern on her face. Michael actually tended to agree with her in this situation.

"No, Ralph's right," Moe said. "He has to be there to clean the stadium anyway. That will help with our cover. We don't want to attract a lot of attention."

"I do. I LOVE attention!" Michael said. "Can Crispin come too?"

"No, Michael, not right now," Mable said. "We have some important stuff to do here at the Sleeve. We just got her back. We don't want to lose her again."

Michael looked at Crispin hopefully. She shrugged.

"They're right, Michael. I think it would be best if you and your brother go."

"But it was going to be a DATE!" Michael said angrily. "You, me...and then Ralph as a chaperone cause we're only thirteen."

Crispin laughed. "Don't worry. We'll have plenty of time for that later. This is kind of a big deal."

"Then it's settled," Moe said, smiling. "Rest up! For tonight is the most important night in Nervous Sleeve history. Tonight is the night we defeat Lord Piper!"

But it's a date with my BROTHER, Michael thought.

"Awwwww NO. Awwwwww NO! NOT YOU AGAIN!!!!! Awwwww NO. Awwwwwwwwwwww NO."

Michael and Ralph were standing on the curb outside Hungry Woody's attempting to get into a cab. Unlike most hard-working cabbies, this driver wouldn't let them in, yelling at top volume through closed doors.

"I KNOW WHAT YOU'RE GOING TO ASK ME TO DO, AND I'M NOT GOING TO DO IT! YOU CAN'T MAKE ME! I DO WHAT I WANT! I'M FAMOUS! AT LEAST I WAS FAMOUS! YOU CAN'T MAKE ME!"

*Actually, we can...*Michael thought, pulling a dollar and a handful of lint out of his pocket. *THIS TIME we're paying customers!* He had found the dollar on the ground.

"What's this guy's problem?" Ralph asked, frowning and pulling on the door handle. The locks clicked shut as the cab driver made a face at them through the window.

171

"YEAH REAL MATURE, 'HOT SHOT.' REAL MATURE!" Michael shouted, sticking his tongue out at the cabbie. "He got cut from the Fright when Razzmatazz bought the team. He wouldn't take me and Boris to the stadium the other day either. I guess they used to be big rivals? I don't know anything about football."

"I do, but this isn't about football," Ralph said, banging his fist on the window and potentially making an inappropriate gesture with his hand (I can't say for sure because this is not an adult book). "Razzmatazz owns the cab company. This dude HAS to let us in! He just HAS to!"

"I know," Michael said, nodding. "Plus, we have money!" He showed Ralph the lint. The dollar had blown away somewhere. Michael frowned.

"Ah sick, Michael!" Ralph said, pushing his hand away. "Where did you get that?!?"

"My hand? I don't know, it kind of came with me," Michael said, confused. "I think it's always been there..."

"No, NOT your hand! The lint!" Ralph said, kicking at the door.

My bellybutton....

"I'M GOING TO PULL AWAY NOW," Hot Shot said, pointing toward the road. "DON'T MAKE THIS ANY MESSIER THAN IT ALREADY IS!!!!"

Michael grabbed Ralph's hand and looked for a watch. When he didn't see one, he went through Ralph's pocket until he found a phone.

*Aha! The time! Hey, wait...*he thought, panicking. *We need to get to the game NOW!*

"Ahhh!!!" Ralph said, grabbing his phone and shuddering. "Leave me alone!"

"I'LL LEAVE YOU ALONE, I'M GOING NOW!" Hot Shot yelled, as he started to turn back onto the road.

"Oh no, you don't!!!!" Michael said angrily.

BLAM! POW! (Old school superhero sounds!)

Hot Shot's cab screeched to a halt, glass falling to the ground. Ralph blinked and looked at his brother. Michael's hand was dripping in blood.

"We're leaving now," Michael said, reaching through the broken window and unlocking the door. "I don't want to miss tailgating, whatever that is."

"Did you just punch through the glass?!?!" Ralph gasped as he followed Michael into the back seat. Michael held up his bloody hand awkwardly, not knowing where to put it. He didn't want to stain his favorite shirt.

Hot Shot stared at them blankly, tears running down his face. "I'm going to have to pay for that!" he said, shaking his head. "I know you don't have any money. You never have money."

Michael held up the lint. It was covered in blood.

Hot Shot took one look at it and began to wail.

"Is that a no?" Michael asked, as they pulled onto the road. *Wow. And it took me THREE WHOLE MONTHS to get this much! I can't believe him! The nerve. Seriously! What is WITH people these days?!?!? Oh, the humanity!* He threw the lint on the ground. They sat in silence.

"So wait, why didn't we take your truck?" Michael asked, staring at his hand. The blood was beginning to dry around a particularly large piece of glass he was too afraid to take out.

"Are you kidding?" Ralph said, laughing. "Parking costs like $50 at the stadium. I'm not paying that."

"But you work there," Michael said, confused. "Don't you just park for free?"

"No way," Ralph said. "Razzmatazz said the only way he can get customers to pay that much is if the employees do too."

"That's awful!" Michael gasped. "At least you get paid for all that cleaning."

"Yeah, like forty bucks," Ralph frowned. "It's like I'm paying him to be there." (You are...)

"Does Razzmatazz pay the $50?" Michael asked.

"Nah, he doesn't have to," Ralph said. "He paid to have his house moved next door. They tore down the Super Duper Save just to do it. Like half the town lost their jobs."

CRASHHHHHHHHHHHHHHHHHH!!!!!! WHAM! WHAM WHAM WHAM! THUMP! THUMP! THUMP! THUMP! THUMP! THUMP! THUMP! THUMP!

"What was that?" Michael gasped, looking around.

They had crashed through the front gate of the stadium and were parked on top of a hot dog stand. The cab was beginning to smoke.

"This is as close as I'm getting," Hot Shot snapped, crossing his arms.

Michael looked at his brother, then down at his blood covered hand. All of the glass had come out on impact. *Cool*, he thought.

"We just broke the front gate!" Ralph said, incredulously. "We're inside the stadium!"

"I know! Talk about service," Michael said brightly. He hadn't been looking forward to fighting the crowds at the entrance.

"But what about those thumps! The other people! I'm going to have to clean this up!" Ralph groaned.

"Ah, you have nothing to complain about," Michael said. "You'll get $40!"

"But...but...." Ralph didn't know what to say.

"It was actually nice driving you guys," Hot Shot said, saluting them. "I'm going to get out of here before I have to pay for parking! Remember...you didn't see me!"

With that, he shot backwards, crashing into the ticket booth. "Oops," he said, winking at them. He shifted the car out of reverse and sped off, scattering the screaming crowd.

Razzmatazz stepped out of the broken ticket hut, looking flustered. "What the devil just happened here?" he asked, lipstick all over his face.

Suddenly, he spotted Michael and Ralph and smiled. He seemed surprised to see them. "Well, hello, there, Number One Fan and stadium worker whose name I don't know! I was beginning to think you'd never show up!"

Oh, we showed up alright, Michael thought, smiling. *In style!* Ralph was still too shocked to be insulted.

"Well, since you're here," Razzmatazz said, looking at Ralph. "Want to clean this up? I can't remember if you're the day guy, or the night guy, but I don't really care."

"I'm the night guy," Ralph glared at Michael.

"Then you're early! FANTASTIC!" Razzmatazz said brightly. "Get to work!"

Michael saw a man carrying a broom and bucket cheer and skip off into the distance.

That must be the day guy, he thought.

Ralph didn't bother arguing. "I'll meet you up there," he said, rolling his eyes.

"I bet you're excited about watching the game from the owner's suite," Razzmatazz said, ushering Michael into an elevator before he could object. "If I may ask, and I will because I'm rich, why did you bring the night guy? I thought you were going to come with your clean shaven friend? He was so cultured!"

Boris? Cultured? Michael shook his head.

(Sure, why not?)

Michael wanted to cry, but decided that it would be a very 'un-football-like' thing to do. He didn't know if he would ever see the bass player again.

"Ah, you just couldn't bear to share the experience with someone else, could you?" Razzmatazz chuckled, painfully nudging Michael in the ribs. "I wouldn't share it either! Keep it to myself," he laughed. Razzmatazz frowned as he jammed the 100 button on the side of the wall.

Michael ignored him. He was too busy thinking about their plan. Or rather, the lack of a plan. It was apparently the most important day in Sleeve history and he had no idea what to do. He shifted uncomfortably, trying to hide his bloody hand behind his back. He would have to wash it when he got to the suite.

"But of COURSE you can't do the coin toss today," Razzmatazz said, shaking his head. "That just won't do. The queen is coming into town, and I don't think she'd be too happy with me if I preempted her with someone else. No, you'll just have to do it some other time and that's final. I'm sorry, Number One Fan. Maybe next time!"

"But..." Michael began. He'd never said he wanted to do the coin toss!!! *Why would you throw away a perfectly good coin anyway?*

"Ah, here we are!" Razzmatazz said happily.

"Floor 100?" Michael asked hopefully.

"No, dear goodness no," Razzmatazz said, waving him off with his hand. "Floor 10! I'm so interested in things with zeroes. Especially when there are many of them," he chuckled. "It reminds me of money! I LOVE money!"

Michael sighed. *Where is his box anyway? Space?* He scratched his head and paused. *Although THAT would be a good way to watch football. I think...*

(No it wouldn't. You couldn't see anything! It would be like watching football, except with your eyes closed, in another room, while doing something else. Not ideal.)

"Twenty! Oh, this is wonderful," Razzmatazz said, pointing to the wall. Only 70 more floors until 100!"

Even I'M smart enough to know that 70 plus 20 isn't 100. It's 95....(No, it's not. It's 90.)

"Thirty! How delightful! Still 70 floors!" (See, that's right THIS time, but it's confusing because his math is wildly inconsistent.)

"Did you know that this elevator has a cookie dispenser?" Razzmatazz asked seriously, pointing to a slot in the wall.

Michael's eyes lit up. "Wait, really?!?!"

"No," Razzmatazz frowned. "I wanted to put one in, but the engineers couldn't figure it out. Can you believe that?"

"Umm...."

"I couldn't either. That's why I pushed them off the roof!" Razzmatazz said, clapping his hands together.

Michael couldn't tell if he was serious, but he made a mental note to never do any shoddy engineering work while at the stadium. *Check,* he thought.

"And finally 100," Razzmatazz said, shaking his head. "That gets better EVERY TIME!"

They walked out of the elevator and nearly bumped into someone. The man had his head down and was walking quickly. It was Josh! Suddenly, the smile on Razzmatazz's face vanished.

"Excuse me, Number One Fan," Razzmatazz said, motioning to Michael. "I need to speak with my associate here. Alone."

Josh shrieked. "Are you sure he can't stay? I kind of like that guy."

"Oh you do?" Razzmatazz asked, scratching his head. "Well...if you die, he can come to your funeral! That's a good compromise! Isn't that right, Number One Fan?"

Michael nodded, hoping he wouldn't have to actually follow through. He hated funerals. So depressing. Plus, everyone was always so matchy-matchy with their black everything. So tacky.

Razzmatazz motioned Michael around the corner. Michael didn't argue. When he was far enough away, he doubled back. Naturally, he was planning on listening in. You know, which is not really a polite thing to do in most circumstances. Oh well...

Razzmatazz slammed Josh up against the wall. The cameraman screamed. "Why is the boy here?!?!?" Razzmatazz yelled angrily. "You had ONE job to do. ONE! I DON'T want him here! I didn't mean to invite him to the box! I thought you were going to kill him! I just want money! MONEY MONEY MONEY MONEY MONEY!

"Tell us how you REALLY feel," Michael muttered, frowning.

"There were some umm...complications?" Josh offered, trembling in fear.

"You're WORTHLESS, do you hear me? WORTHLESS!" Razzmatazz yelled, looking around to make sure no one was listening. "You make this right," he whispered pointing a finger in Josh's face. "You make this right." Razzmatazz let the cameraman go and brushed off his suit. He started to walk toward the box, but paused. "AND TAKE A SHOWER!!!!!" he shouted.

Michael wheeled around, hoping he wouldn't get caught listening in. Josh had gotten off pretty easy with just a death threat. His heart beat quickly as he ran down the hall. *This isn't working!* he thought. He was even slower when he tried to run. (Now, THAT is an accomplishment!)

Suddenly, the crowd erupted outside. Michael looked through the window. The game was beginning!

"Having trouble finding the box?" Razzmatazz asked, walking up beside him.

Michael jumped. "Umm...I was just admiring the wallpaper?" he said, hoping there actually WAS wallpaper. He had been too busy trying to figure out if the Mona Lisa was a man or a woman to get a lot out of art class.

Razzmatazz smiled. "I do too," he chuckled. "It's gold leaf! Can you believe it?!?!"

Michael sighed in relief. "That's wonderful," he said. He didn't really care. They stood in silence as the start of the pregame video began to blast out over the crowd.

Wait a second...WHAT? Michael thought, confused. Crispin's face was staring up at him from the screen. And Miss Dandelion's. *WHAT'S GOING ON?!?!? I didn't know they were movie stars!* he thought, angrily. *Why wasn't I invited to this?* The picture was grainy and dark like it had been filmed at a warehouse. *Oh....OH!!!!!*

"But that's the beauty of it," Josh said (on screen). "Razzmatazz can continue his job with the news station, while being the beloved owner of Some Town's favorite team. They'll never suspect he's working with a secret organization, providing funds for inhumane experiments and plotting his own violent and greedy takeover of the town. It's just perfect!"

As confusion swept over the crowd, Razzmatazz smiled, an eerie calm on his face.

I think I'd rather he be angry...

"Change of plans," Razzmatazz said. "The game is going to be called on account of murder." He chuckled and took an enormous gun out of his pocket.

You probably think you know what comes next. After all, Razzmatazz is standing in front of Michael with basically a rocket launcher. He wants Michael dead, and they're alone in the hallway. What could be more perfect?

But you're forgetting something. Priorities. It's always about priorities! Michael wasn't in the video. He wasn't responsible for the video. It's not directly his fault that Razzmatazz's evil plan has been revealed to the world and he's now on the run. So whose fault is it?

That's right...Josh.

"Out of my way, spectator!" Razzmatazz yelled, pushing Michael aside and running down the hallway. He was shooting into the air and screaming like they did in the Wild West.

You're probably NOW wondering why Razzmatazz didn't shoot Michael and THEN go after Josh. Wouldn't that have been easier? Yes, but he wouldn't have had enough bullets to shoot into the air. Just go with it.

Michael froze, wondering what he should do next. He didn't like being separated from his brother, especially now that things had gotten sticky. Knowing that it probably wasn't safe for thirteen-year-olds on the concourse, he decided to do the only thing he could think of....eat.

The owner's box was deserted when Michael walked in. *Perfect*, he thought. *More for me!*

There was SO MUCH FOOD! Snappy's Colorful Rainbow Chips, Mr. Sugar's Choco Squares, Mr. Sugar's Vanilla Squares and something else he didn't recognize which looked great. He was in luck! And super hungry...

*Mmmm...*he thought, stuffing his face and watching the scene unfold below.

"I can't believe these people!" he muttered to himself, opening the box of something he didn't recognize. "Football isn't violent, so why is everyone fighting?"

After the video played, the crowd had gone crazy! Fright fans were arguing over whether the accusations were true. Nowhere Knights fans were mocking them and partying. And others were just fighting because they had an excuse. Michael wondered where Razzmatazz was and if Josh was safe.

Suddenly, the door to the suite opened.

"Please, don't shoot!" Michael yelled, throwing the box at the intruder and diving under a buffet table.

"MICHAEL?" Ralph asked, ducking. "Is that you?"

"Ralph?" Michael said, still under the table. "What are you doing? How did you get here?"

"Well, I came to find you," Ralph said, kneeling down so he could see his brother. "And I took the stairs." He shook his head. Michael had chocolate all over his face.

"There's stairs?" Michael said, flabbergasted. "What kind of stadium IS this?"

"One that's surprisingly up to fire code," Ralph said, shaking his head. "Here." He offered his brother a hand. "Hey, wait a second...what's that you're eating?"

"I don't know," Michael said, shrugging. "Is it bad? Am I allergic?" He didn't FEEL any puffier than usual. Not that he could really tell. He was usually pretty puffy...

Ralph grabbed the box and laughed. "You'll be fine, but look!"

Michael snatched the box away from him and gasped. "Mr. Magnificent's Cheesecake Bites! But Mr. Magnificent is the DIRECT COMPETITOR to Mr. Sugar! Holy CROW! I'm a brand loyalist. I can't believe I ate these!" He coughed and spat dramatically on the ground.

"Were they good?" Ralph asked, smiling.

"Umm...yes..." Michael admitted. "Hey, we've got to get out of here!"

"That's not going to be easy," Ralph said, looking down at the concourse. The mascot was defending itself with a t-shirt gun. "Do you think our contact is still here?"

Of course!!! Michael thought, horrified.

He'd forgotten all about the real reason they were at the game. *NOT food...NOT food...*"I don't know," he said. "If it's someone we know, we might be able to find them?"

(Good thinking...)

"But if it's not?" Ralph asked, grabbing a handful of Cheesecake Bites.

"DON'T EVEN THINK ABOUT IT!" Michael said angrily, slapping the box away.

Ralph cringed. Michael's hand was still covered in dried blood. "Okay, let's go. We don't want to go back to the Sleeve empty-handed."

"Don't worry!" Michael said. "We won't."

Ralph looked over at his brother and sighed. Michael had shoved the remaining boxes of Mr. Sugar's products into his pants. Or had he? Maybe he was just big...

"I'm not taking the stairs either," Michael said. "Too much downhill walking. It's bad for my digestion."

"Whatever," Ralph said.

When they got to the elevator, they were horrified to find Josh's body blocking the way. He was dead. That's why he was described as a body.

"Do you think HE was the one who played the video?" Ralph asked, carefully stepping over the cameraman and pressing the 'down' button.

"Nah, there's no way!" Michael said through mouthfuls of cookies. "You should have seen the argument

189

he had with Razzmatazz before the game. I just can't see him doing that when his life was in danger!"

"But maybe that's WHY he did it?" Ralph said, as the doors opened. "Maybe he was tired of working for Razzmatazz. You know, like, doing the wrong thing?"

"Maybe," Michael said.

"Either way, it didn't really end up all that great for him," Ralph said, shaking his head.

"At least he didn't get pushed off the roof," Michael muttered.

"What?!?" Ralph asked.

"HEY GUYS!" someone yelled.

Michael's heart skipped a beat. *Razzmatazz?!?*

It was Hot Shot. He was getting out of the elevator as they were getting in.

"What the hey are you doing here?" Michael asked.

Hot Shot chuckled. "I heard about what happened and came back to gloat. When I couldn't find Razzmatazz, I figured I would just come up here and trash the place."

"You have fun, man," Ralph said, looking at Michael and shrugging as they entered the elevator. "Don't go too crazy. You might have to pay for it!"

Hot Shot looked at them and started laughing. "I think I might be back on the team now, so it doesn't really matter, does it?"

The doors closed, and Michael and Ralph began their descent back toward the lobby.

"Do you think he's mentally stable?" Michael asked, as a pile of crumbs fell down his shirt. He'd already eaten half of the boxes from the buffet.

"Let's not stick around and find out," Ralph said.

DING!

Ah, crap, floor 90, Michael thought.

"That was fast," Ralph said, stepping out of the elevator. "Let's go."

Michael blinked and looked at his brother. He was right, they were already there. "FLOOR 1! WHAT?!?" he yelled. "I DON'T UNDERSTAND THE LAWS OF TIME AND SPACE!" Michael was irate.

"Sometimes, I just don't understand you," Ralph said, frowning.

"That's because I'm...LIEUTENANT PAUL?!?!?!?" Michael shouted, slapping his face. *Confound it! Ow!*

"No, you're not," Ralph said, looking for a safe way to the front gate. A row of bleachers flew over their heads and crashed into the elevator behind them.

"What?" Michael asked. "No, I was about to say something else, and then I saw Lieutenant Paul! SEE!"

Ralph looked at where his brother was pointing and sure enough, it was the gorilla! He was standing alone, a few sections away from them, scanning the crowd.

"But how? Why? When?" Ralph wanted to ask more questions, but figured that Michael probably didn't know the answers anyway. "Isn't he dead?!?"

"Maybe not," Michael said, considering the fact that Paul COULD possibly be a ghost, or some kind of spirit. "Maybe he only pretended to be dead? I'm sure he has his reasons. Wait a second...maybe he's our CONTACT!" He ran to the gorilla, yelling excitedly. "PAUL!!! PAUL!!! PAUL!!! PAUL!!! PAUL!!! PAUL!!! PAUL!!! PAUL!!!"

"That would actually make ME want to run in the opposite direction," Ralph muttered.

But it did the trick. The gorilla spotted them and started to come their way. It wasn't until he was almost upon them that Michael realized something was wrong. Something was different. Lieutenant Paul's eyes were red. And he looked angry.

BUT I CAN'T STOP!!! Michael thought, having finally gotten the hang of running.

He ducked just in time, narrowly avoiding the swipe of Paul's arm. Ralph, having started later, but run faster, collided with Paul and crashed to the ground.

"It's a TRAP!!!" Ralph yelled, as Paul grabbed him around the legs.

Michael couldn't believe it. He'd spent months hoping his friend wasn't dead, but now that he wasn't, Michael wanted to take it back. Had Paul tricked them into coming to the stadium? Was HE the one who had shown the wrong pregame video? Had he faked his own death so he could work for Lord Piper?

Did he prefer Mr. Magnificent to Mr. Sugar?

"A little help," Ralph gasped, as Paul pinned him to the ground.

Michael frowned and crossed his arms. *Where IS Sneaky Pete when you need him?!?* he wondered, beginning to doubt the reliability of his childhood hero.

Suddenly, the scoreboard came crashing through the wall, hitting the gorilla squarely on the chest and knocking him out. It missed Ralph's head by inches.

"THAT FELT REALLY GOOD!" Hot Shot yelled, running past them. Michael guessed they would probably have to take a different cab home.

"Come on!" Ralph said, grabbing Michael and running toward the gate.

But Michael felt like he was moving in slow motion. Had Paul been fooling them all this time? Had the Sleeve been thinking that they were the ones getting secrets, when it was really Lord Piper? He didn't want to go back to headquarters because he wasn't sure everyone could recover from the devastating news. Not this time.

I just won't tell them, he decided. *We'll explain what happened with the video and say we weren't able to meet our contact.* But Michael felt bad for lying, even though he hadn't done it yet. He's just not that kind of guy.

You shouldn't be either. Even if you're not a guy!

Something made Michael pause when they got to the gate. "Is that? Wait a second...it CAN'T be!" he said.

"Michael, COME ON!" Ralph shouted as sirens blared urgently in the background. Apparently, the manhunt had begun for Some Town's local hero.

"Ralph, it's Tugley, LOOK!"

But the turtle was already gone.

"It's not him, Michael," Ralph said. "And besides, even if it was, he's bad news."

"I guess you're right," Michael said, shaking his head. He was SURE he'd seen Tugley. But what was he doing here? Michael followed Ralph into the parking lot. Most of the tailgaters seemed unaware of what was going on inside the stadium. Which wasn't a surprise to anyone.

"I guess we'll just have to go to another game," Michael chuckled, weaving his way through the crowd. "Right Ralph?"

But Ralph didn't answer him. Michael turned and saw that he had fallen to the ground. "Ralph, are you okay?" he asked, guessing that his brother had tripped. Many of the tailgaters were stumbling around as well for some reason.

But Ralph hadn't tripped. Something else was going on. Something bad! As Ralph's eyes glazed over, he began to shake violently in place. Michael screamed.

The serum!!!

It was Michael's worst nightmare! Well, sort of. He wasn't being attacked by clowns on unicorns or cupcake spiders, but it was LIKE his worst nightmare. Ralph was changing before his eyes!

As Michael's brother began to grow in size, thick, blue fur sprouted all over him. He looked up at Michael and growled, a hungry look in his eyes.

If THIS is puberty, count me out, Michael thought, covering his mouth because that's what you're supposed to do when you're scared.

He backed up, looking around for something to defend himself with. Unfortunately, all of the guns, knives and throwing stars had been confiscated at the gate. That left him with just his hands and his ingenuity to fight with.

I'm dead. Definitely, absolutely, positively dead. Well, life, you've been fun. Thanks for thirteen great years!

Michael shook his head. He didn't even know how to punch! Or chop! Or really do anything violent. He stared at his hands, trying to brainstorm something that would help. He figured Monster Ralph wouldn't be impressed by all the dried blood on his fingers.

It looks like I've been playing in the sandbox!

(Yeah. Not all that impressive. Sorry, man.)

Ralph was STILL GROWING. He was now bigger than the team bus and it didn't look like he was stopping anytime soon.

"Wait until Mom sees this!" Michael muttered. "Maybe she'll be too busy to be mad? Or the other option. She might blame me, and I don't see how this is my fault."

Monster Ralph moved in and Michael jumped to the side. "TAKE THAT!" he yelled, before realizing he'd uttered a phrase that was usually reserved for when you actually did something (not for when you dove out of the way and nothing happened). Michael frowned, realizing he was in a stickier situation than he'd thought.

On cue, Ralph reared his head back and roared, cracking the pavement and creating a sinkhole. It was epic.

Well, THAT'S kind of scary, Michael thought, quickly unlatching his fanny pack. *I knew this would come in handy some day.*

Ralph made the first move, charging at Michael. The ground shook beneath them, making Ralph unsteady on his feet.

Wow, it looks like he's as inexperienced being a monster as I am using my fanny pack as a weapon! Michael thought, dodging to the side.

Despite his weight, Michael found it easy to avoid Ralph's attacks. His brother was slow, and he didn't have as much space to move around in. "I'm incredible!" he chuckled, making a mental note to get in more fights.

But Monster Ralph proved to be a quick learner. He turned around and in no time, had backed Michael into a corner. *It may be time to use the 'pack,'* he thought. Michael still didn't REALLY want to kill Ralph, but he may not have a choice.

Ralph screamed and lunged at him.

Holy crow, that was close! Michael thought, diving to the ground to avoid an overhead swipe. As he looked up to reposition himself, blood dripped into his eye. Michael's heart stopped. *OH MY GOODNESS, I'VE BEEN HIT!!!!!!*

He stood up, staggering. *This is it. I'm going to be killed by a monster version of my own brother! If this happened to anyone else it might be cool. Right now, it's decidedly un-cool. Or, not cool. Or, whatever.*

Ralph jumped. Michael screamed. And suddenly, Ralph was knocked to the side, falling to the ground unconscious! Michael stopped screaming to see what was going on.

It was BORIS!!! The bass player had come out of nowhere, saving Michael just in time.

"Well, that was easy," Boris laughed, putting his foot on top of Ralph. You know, like people do when they conquer something. You've seen it.

The bass player frowned and looked at the bottom of his shoe. He shook his head and wiped it off with his sleeve before putting it back. "That's better," he said.

"How in the world did you do that?" Michael asked. He latched his fanny pack back onto his waist. *Good thing I was never serious about using this anyway!*

"Oh, it's easy, really," Boris said proudly, running his hand through his close cropped hair. "When you're a champion." He flashed Michael a brilliant smile.

"I thought you were dead?" Michael frowned.

"Well, coming back from the dead isn't all that hard...when you're a champion."

Michael shook his head. "You weren't actually dead, were you?"

"Not that I know of," Boris said, shrugging. "But most of the time, my stories are a LOT more interesting if I just make them up."

"That's not very honest though," Michael said, disapprovingly.

"I'd never thought of it THAT way," Boris said, scratching his head. "And anyway, I just wanted to use my new catch phrase! I add 'when you're a champion' to the end of stuff! It's the best catch phrase since right now."

"I'm pretty sure THAT'S not true," Michael said.

He'd been preparing to use 'anything with puppets is better than anything without puppets' for a while, he just hadn't been given the chance yet. Now he may never get to. What a cruel world we live in...

"Whatever," Boris said. "We need to get Ralph some help. I went through this on a smaller scale, but from what I can tell, Ralph got a larger dose of whatever that stuff was. How many syringes did they inject him with?"

"At least five," Michael said, concerned. He wiped his face. Apparently, he had a nose bleed. *Aha! Blood!*

"That's worse than I thought," Boris said. "I can only count to four, so I'd hoped that they'd stopped at that. We need to move him to safety."

"Will he come out of it?" Michael asked as they walked around, trying to figure out how to carry the unconscious monster.

"Oh, probably," Boris said reassuringly. "Things are going our way now. Look!" He held up one of Lord Piper's necklaces.

"Whose is that?" Michael asked, hoping the bass player had somehow traveled to Lord Piper's secret hideout and confronted the fox before coming back to help him with Ralph. Wishful thinking.

"It's the Cardinal cardinal's," Boris smiled.

"DRAT!" Michael said angrily before correcting himself. "I mean, awesome!"

"That's not all though," Boris said, confused. "I'm sure you were wondering who showed the video at the stadium?"

"Well, I was, but then I kind of forgot about it," Michael said truthfully.

Boris frowned. "It was ME! I stole it from Josh and put it up there!"

Michael stared at him in disbelief. "How could you have done that if you were off fighting Lord Piper?!?!" *He's bluffing...he's got to be.*

"What?" Boris asked. "I didn't fight Lord Piper. And anyway, it wasn't that hard. Espionage is easy...when you're a champion."

Ralph grunted and rolled over.

"Whoa...we need to get this dude out of here," Boris said. He looked at Michael's scrawny arms and shook his head. "Don't worry, I've got this."

"But where can we go?" Michael asked, as they walked down the street. He wasn't offended that Boris didn't want his help. He was off the hook!

"The only thing open this time of night is Black Orb," Boris sighed.

"What's that?" Michael asked. "I'm probably too young for that kind of thing, right?"

"Definitely yes," Boris laughed, grunting under the weight of Monster Ralph. "It's a nightclub. And not a KID nightclub either."

"Will they let me in?" Michael asked. He didn't want to leave Ralph until he was better.

"That actually depends on a lot of things," Boris said, opening the door to the Orb.

"What do you mean?" Michael asked.

"It's owned by Lord Piper..." Boris said, trailing off.

Michael gasped.

"Long time, no see, gentleman," Jerry Mudwater drawled, a smile on his face.

Michael turned around , but an enormous guard was blocking the door. They'd walked into a trap!

"Well, aren't you going to say you missed me too?" Jerry asked, winking. He looked at them and smiled, pausing when he saw the monster on Boris' back. "What IS that? You know we don't allow weapons in the club!"

"It's not a weapon, it's my brother!" Michael said angrily. He'd already beaten up Jerry in his heart.

Unfortunately, that didn't count.

"I'm just kidding," Jerry laughed, pulling his suit coat aside to reveal a shotgun. "See?"

That looks uncomfortable, Michael thought. *It creates that awkward bulge in his pants!*

"We're not here to make small talk, bro!" Boris said, looking for somewhere to put Ralph down. "We need help!

This guy got injected with stuff! Like, weird stuff and we don't know what it is! A three-legged cat did it!"

"Oh, did he?" Jerry asked, a look of mock concern on his face. He rubbed his goatee, deep in thought. "Well, why didn't you say so? Come on back, friends!" He motioned for them to follow him deeper into the club, walking with a spring in his step.

I'm not sure I can respect a guy who hops, Michael thought, catching himself about to do the same thing. *Drat!* He turned around, hoping to escape, but the guard growled at him.

Literally growled. Like an untrained, wild baboon.

Eeeeek! Michael thought, deciding it would be best to just follow Jerry. Ralph's life may depend on it. And his own. And probably Boris'. But definitely Ralph's.

The bass player looked at him and Michael shrugged. "I guess we don't have a choice, bro," Boris said, adjusting Ralph on his back and following Jerry down the hall. Ralph stirred, but didn't wake up.

Michael glared at the guard. "You can use words, you know! You're a PERSON."

The guard smiled.

Michael sighed and followed the others through the club. It was unlike anything he'd ever seen! If he didn't know it was owned by Lord Piper, he might have planned a return trip when he turned 18. It was that cool! Seriously.

I'm REALLY feeling this music, he thought, closing his eyes. The pulsing rhythm resonated deeply in his heart.

Now, it's a bad idea to close your eyes when you're walking somewhere because then it's harder to see where you're going. But it's a REALLY bad idea to close your eyes when you're walking somewhere NEW because then you're likely to bump into something. Or someone. Which is exactly what happened.

"OWWW! JUNK! GARBAGE!" Michael yelled.

The music stopped and everyone turned to look at him. *This happens wayyyyyyyyy too often*, he thought, shaking his head. *Who's writing this book?!?*

In his excitement, he'd bumped into a cocktail waitress carrying a plate of colorful drinks. Somehow, he'd managed to stay dry, but the same could not be said for the waitress. Her octopus schoolgirl outfit was soaked!

"THAT'S IT!" she screamed. "I'M going to go work at a respectable place like The Flamingo Room!" She pushed past Michael, storming out of the club.

"She'll be back," Jerry chuckled, as the music started again. "This happens every night."

"Really?" Michael asked, trying to control his 'dance reflex.' "How do you know?"

"There's just something about this place," Jerry said. "It really draws you in, you know? It's one of my greatest accomplishments. Also, Lord Piper threatened to kill her family. She's the only one that can fit in the octopus outfit and the customers really like it."

"I like it too," the guard said, nodding his head.

Michael turned around. "Aha! You CAN talk!"

The guard took a step forward and growled at him.

"This IS a pretty nice club," Boris said, changing the subject. "I know I'm not supposed to say that because you're a bad guy, but it's true."

"Am I?" Jerry asked as they entered the back room. "What IS a bad guy, really?"

Michael fist bumped himself. He hadn't knocked into anything else!

"You dudes are bad guys!" Boris said, looking around. "You've trapped us in a bigger trap!"

"Have a seat," Jerry laughed, motioning for them to sit on a couple of beanbags in the corner.

They entered a dark, smoky room with a low ceiling- probably Jerry's office. Two men were sitting at a table, playing cards and laughing. Michael frowned. One of them looked VERY familiar.

"Principal Goodburn?" he gasped, pulling his beanbag over to the action. His head barely came over the top of the table.

"Why, Mr. Pumpernickel! It's SO nice to see you!" Principal Goodburn said, stroking a goose on his lap. "But you know, I'm not a principal anymore. I'm the Superintendant of Some Town School District!" He looked genuinely happy to see them.

"Of course you are," the second, larger, man laughed, waving his cigar in Michael's face. "He's probably just too stupid to know that. No offense," he added.

"Now, wait a second," Principal Goodburn said, getting red in the face. "That sounds like an unfair critique of my school system! Mr. Pumpernickel isn't THAT stupid! Are you, Mr. Pumpernickel? Either way, he's hardly representative of the intelligence of the general student population."

What does he mean by THAT? Michael thought. *I haven't even been to school in months except for that one time which doesn't even really count all that much!*

"No one is saying you're doing a poor job, Lionel!" Jerry drawled, shaking his head. "It's just Doogie being Doogie. Forget about it."

"I'm serious!" Principal Goodburn said, startling the goose and causing it to fly away. "I earned my position! I'm good at what I do!"

"Right," Doogie laughed, slapping the table. "And Lord Piper had nothing to do with it?"

Jerry glared at him, clenching his fists. "ENOUGH. Let's get down to business."

"You know how I loveeeeeee business!" Doogie laughed. "Business is my middle name!"

"No it's NOT!" Principal Goodburn snapped. He glanced around, looking for the goose.

"It actually is," Doogie said, shrugging. He adjusted his fedora. Its royal blue color reminded Michael of a certain school he didn't like.

You know which one I'm talking about.

"BROS, WE NEED YOUR HELP!" Boris shouted.

The bass player was standing in the corner next to Ralph. Michael's brother was tossing and turning, showing no signs of waking up.

"What the devil is that?" Doogie said, falling out of his chair. "Doggone it!" He picked up his hat and stuffed it back onto his head. "It's just so ugly, no offense."

"That's Mr. Pumpernickel's brother," Jerry said, pointing at Michael. "They came here for help because Mr. Pumpernickel got injected by the agents of Dexterum Dei."

"The Resistance?" Principal Goodburn gulped. "Are they on the move?"

"Dexterum Dei isn't the Resistance, the Nervous Sleeve is, you nitwit!" Doogie chuckled, picking his cigar off the ground and sitting back in his chair. "That stupid cat is just a distraction."

"That stupid cat is DANGEROUS!" Jerry said angrily, glaring at Doogie. "I think Mr. Pumpernickel's current predicament confirms that."

"Seems fine to me," Doogie said, looking at Michael.

"Not that Mr. Pumpernickel, the OTHER ONE!" Jerry shouted, pulling a chunk of hair out of his mullet.

"If you don't watch out, you'll be ugly like Lionel," Doogie laughed. "No offense."

"JUST STOP!!!!" Michael yelled, his voice echoing around the room. He was tired of it! Ralph needed help. Bad guys, or no bad guys, he was determined to make something good come out of this.

"Who said that?!?" Doogie asked, looking around.

"I think it was Mr. Pumpernickel," Principal Goodburn said, beckoning the goose to sit on his lap.

"Isn't he passed out?" Doogie asked, dumbfounded. He looked over at Ralph.

"Not THAT Mr. Pumpernickel, the other one!" Principal Goodburn snapped.

"If you're, like, not going to help us, at least tell us what's going on," Boris said. "Who are these guys and why are they here?"

"I apologize, I've been rude," Jerry said. "Michael, you know, Lionel."

"Hi," Principal Goodburn said, waving.

"Well, this is Doogie Bluestone, Some Town School District Athletic Director." He pointed to the large man with the hat.

"Much obliged," Doogie said, lighting another cigar. He blew a large puff of smoke in Michael's face.

"Wait...Lord Piper has infiltrated sports too?" Michael coughed. He couldn't imagine a world where athletics were corrupt! That just wouldn't make any sense!!!

Doogie laughed. "You're not the brightest bulb in the box, are you, no offense?" he asked.

This man makes me angry, Michael thought.

"Lord Piper is everywhere," Jerry shrugged, taking out a glass and pouring some whiskey. "He's going to help me become mayor!"

"I WON'T VOTE FOR YOU!" Boris frowned.

"Of course not," Jerry chuckled. "You're not even in the country legally, are you?"

What?!?!

Boris shifted uncomfortably.

"Anyway," Jerry laughed, "he made Lionel here Superintendent. He made Doogie Athletic Director. He even made all THREE of us the owners of this club! All we had to do was agree to help him anytime he needed it. He's a pretty hands-off guy, so it's quite the arrangement."

"But how can you work for someone who's so evil?" Michael asked, this time raising his voice so he could be heard from under the table.

"Lord Piper isn't evil, Michael," Principal Goodburn said, shaking his head. "He's a hero! He wants what's best for this town!"

"He wants what's best for HIM!" Boris said.

"I can see how you'd think that," Jerry said. "But look at the people who are REALLY harming our city. People like Razzmatazz and that cat!"

"The cat IS bad," Michael said.

"Don't agree with them!" Boris shouted.

"Boris, it's OKAY. I know you've worked with Lord Piper before. Didn't you see it? Didn't you see the great work he's trying to do?" Jerry asked.

"All I see right now is a friend in need and a bunch of guys who are stopping me from getting the care he deserves," Boris said angrily.

"But we ARE helping him," Jerry said, shaking his head. "We're helping YOU. While you guys were arguing, I called Lord Piper. He's on the way."

"WHAT?" Michael shouted, jumping off of his beanbag and falling to the floor.

Doogie started to laugh. "Boy, you don't play sports in school, do you, no offense?"

"It depends what a sport is," Michael said, brushing his shirt off, embarrassed. "Is freestyle acapella a sport?"

"What?!?!" Doogie asked, confused. "No."

"What about practicing vocal intervals?"

"NO!" Doogie said, dousing his cigar on Principal Goodburn's leg.

"AHHHHHHHH!!!!" the Superintendent screamed.

"What about epic musical composition?"

"NO! I DON'T EVEN KNOW WHAT THAT IS!!!"

"Is it so wrong to have a song in my heart?" Michael asked. He was determined to defend the honor of his only afterschool activity.

"I guess not?" Doogie said, scratching his head.

"Good!" Michael smiled, beginning to sing.

"Y'all need to calm down," Jerry said, pulling a big can of 'goatee wax' out of his desk. "Lord Piper should be here any minute!"

"I hope he brings a sample of that new necklace he's been working on," Doogie coughed, putting his feet on the table. "It's supposed to be even BETTER than the first one."

Jerry glared at him. "It's also supposed to be a secret right now!"

"It's okay, bro, we knew about it," Boris shrugged.

"It's going to turn the tides for good," Jerry said, putting a large dab of wax on his goatee. "Oh, how he'll reward me when he gets here."

"You mean reward US, Jerry!" Principal Goodburn said, hopefully.

"I mean ME!" Jerry snapped, shaking his head.

RING! RING! RING! RING! RING! RING! RING! RING! RING! RING! RING! RING! RING! RING! RING!

Is that a phone? Michael wondered. *It's too conventional for Boris...*

"That must be him!" Jerry said, a smile on his face. "Yes?" he asked, answering the call. "Yes. No. DON'T BE STUPID, WE ALWAYS MEET HIM IN THE BACK! Yes. Stop growling at me and send him back here!"

Jerry threw his phone on the desk in disgust. It landed on a folder labeled "Important Potentially Incriminating Documents," knocking it to the floor.

Michael wasn't sure what 'incriminating' meant, but he picked up the folder anyway and stuffed it in his fanny pack. It could come in handy for his next book report.

"That guy is so dumb," Jerry scoffed, quickly flattening the back of his hair. "Why did we hire him?"

"I thought he was your cousin?" Doogie frowned.

"I thought he was Lord Piper's cousin," Principal Goodburn said, shrugging. "He acts like an animal. Not that there's anything wrong with that."

"GRRRRRR SNARLLLL GRR! SNARL! GRR!"

"See what I mean?!?" Principal Goodburn said, holding out his hands. "We can even hear him from here! He needs some manners!"

"That's no animal," Doogie said, backing up towards the wall. "And it's no body guard either! It's Mr. Pumpernickel!"

Everyone turned to see what he was looking at. Ralph had woken up! Michael's brother was standing in the corner, holding his head. No one moved.

"Michael," Ralph said, breathing heavily.

"Ralph?" Michael asked, starting to cry. Somewhere beneath the monster, Ralph was fighting a losing battle to take control of his own body.

"You and Boris have to get out of here," Ralph said, gasping for air. "Lord Piper is coming. I'll handle them."

"We're not leaving you, bro!" Boris said, looking shocked as he started to cry himself.

"Of course you're not!" Jerry said with disgust. "If you leave, I can't be rewarded for capturing you!"

"Thank you for everything you've done," Ralph said, coughing. "But please, go." He clutched the wall and lowered his head. The monster had returned.

"Boris, it's now or never!" Michael said. The bad guys looked on, too speechless to move.

"We can't leave Ralph!" Boris cried, shaking his head. "He's too important!"

"It's too late," Michael said, sadly. "It's what he would want."

Monster Ralph growled and charged across the room. Michael and Boris ran past him in the other direction, bolting through the door and back into the club. They could hear Jerry's screaming as they ran through the crowd, not daring to turn back.

There was no sign of Lord Piper anywhere! They must have just missed him! Probably because he was coming to the back door. He ALWAYS comes to the back door.

"That was close!" Boris said as they burst back on the street. "But now what?"

They stopped outside the Orb, gasping for breath.

Michael smiled, a look of determination on his face. "We have to go to the police station," he said, pulling a folder labeled 'Important, Potentially Incriminating Documents' out of his pocket. "It appears that our friends at the Orb obtained the club in an illegal way. Not only that, but they haven't been paying their taxes!"

"That was the shortest visit I'VE ever taken to the police station," Boris said as they walked up the hill toward Hungry Woody's.

"Do I want to know?" Michael asked, smiling.

"Nah, probably not, but I'd love to tell you sometime," Boris chuckled.

Not a chance, Michael thought. *Not a chance...*

They walked into the restaurant to thunderous applause. Michael beamed, feeling pretty good about himself.

"Thank you, thank you," he said, bowing and waving. "Thank you."

This is the greatest thing that's ever happened to me since the last time I said this! he thought, smiling at how great his day was despite the fact that his brother was probably dead. When he was done bowing, and his waving hand was tired, he looked up and frowned. There was no one there!

Who applauded?

"I think they're in the other room watching 'Vampires Destroying Big Things in a Big Way,'" Boris shrugged. "Come on, I don't want to miss it either. Today's episode must be pretty good."

I bet my dad is watching this, Michael thought, as they entered the kitchen.

No one heard them come in because they were all glued to the show. Michael spotted a bag of Rainbow Chips and immediately began to dig in.

"We watch the vampire in his natural habitat. He creeps silently along the city streets, a pensive look on his face. This isn't his first kill, nor will it be his last. But this particular location holds a special significance to this vampire. Yes! This is where his life changed forever. It's where he first experienced the sweet taste of blood. Warm, human blood. It's where he became a vampire..."

CRUNCH!

Michael had been trying to chew quietly, but eating loudly was one of his hobbies. Panicking, he shoved the rest of the chips in his mouth, bag and all.

CRUNCH! CRUNCH! CRUNCH! CRUNCH! CRUNCH! CRUNCH! CRINKLE! That was the bag!

"MICHAEL!" Schumer said, spotting them in the doorway and knocking over his friend.

"The vampire attacks with quick precision and an empty conscious..."

"Owww. Junk. Trash. Schumer, nice to see you too," Michael grunted.

Schumer apologized and turned to Boris, his eyes wide. "BORIS, YOU'RE ALIVE! I CAN'T BELIEVE IT! EVERYBODY, LOOK!" He started to run towards the bass player, but Boris held up his hand and shook his head.

"I got this," Boris said, falling backwards and groaning like he'd been hit too.

"The vampire sometimes exhibits strange habits in an attempt to impress others..."

"That's just weird," Michael said.

"Weird, but wonderful!" Moe said happily, as the others turned their attention away from the TV. "Boris, we thought you were gone! What happened?"

"Well," the bass player said, running his hand through his close cropped hair. "Nothing is difficult...when you're a champion." He winked at Ms. Jones, who blushed and motioned for him to meet her in the next room.

"Where's Ralph?" Miss Dandelion asked, looking behind them. "Why isn't he with you guys?"

Michael hung his head. He couldn't bring himself to say anything about his brother.

"Yeah, about that," Boris said, starting to break down. He couldn't handle it. The bass player collapsed onto the ground, knocking the TV sideways on its stand.

"QUIET DOWN, I'M WATCHING THIS!" Cephas yelled, adjusting it back to its original position.

Everyone glared at him.

"What?" the mole asked, shaking his head.

"Boris, it's alright!" Stan said, helping the bass player into a chair. "Tell us what happened, we'll listen!"

He nodded hopefully, pulling his vest down over his bulging stomach.

Boris took a deep breath, knowing he was about to say the hardest thing he'd ever said in his whole life. "I think Ralph's gone, guys." He grabbed Stan's vest and blew his nose loudly.

The dog trainer frowned and hopped backwards, almost bumping into Miss Dandelion.

"What do you mean, gone?" Miss Dandelion asked, snatching Stan's vest and blowing her nose too. Don't worry, it was in a different place. It was SO big, after all!

Stan squealed, ripping his vest off and throwing it across the room. "Germs!" he yelled.

Boris frowned. Sighing, he explained everything that had happened at the stadium, from the video about Razzmatazz, to their encounter with Jerry and the others. When he was done, the room was silent, except for the sound of noses blowing. Everyone had a piece of Stan's vest. Naturally, they were passing it around.

"I'm SO sorry," Crispin said, walking over and placing her hand on Michael's back.

Michael nodded, but didn't say anything. By acknowledging Ralph's death, he would have to admit that it had actually happened.

He couldn't do that.

No one else had the energy to say anything either. They'd lost friends before, but somehow, this was different. Ralph hadn't died at the hands of Lord Piper, he'd died at the hands of someone else. Another threat.

Ralph hadn't even wanted to be part of this fight. Many of them had joined voluntarily, but Michael's brother had only participated to protect the ones he loved. As they sat in silence, the television continued to blare in the background.

"The vampire moves in for the kill. Here he is, on the verge of his greatest accomplishment to date. If successful, this will be the biggest thing he's ever destroyed. He begins the countdown to destruction. 3...2...

Suddenly, the screen turned black before cutting to Cindy Wallace in the News Channel 90613 newsroom.

"We interrupt whatever important thing you've been watching to bring you an exclusive update on the increasing crime in Some Town. We will not be cutting back to your show. We will discuss what we're about to say for another hour and a half. We are not sorry for the inconvenience because crime doesn't care."

"BLAST IT ALL! WE'VE MISSED THE BEST PART!" a voice yelled from somewhere outside the room.

Dad?!?!? Michael wondered, horrified.

"Like, who was that?" Boris asked, wiping his eyes.

"That was my DAD!" Michael said, looking around.

"Please be quiet, dear, we need to hear this!" Mable said, waving a towel in their direction.

"Prominent businessman Jerry Mudwater has been arrested today for obtaining property in an illegal manner. Mudwater, along with business partners, Some Town School District Superintendent Lionel Goodburn and Athletic Director Doogie Bluestone, have pleaded not guilty for their involvement in the purchase of Some Town's trendiest nightclub, the Black Orb. Last night, the Orb was mysteriously destroyed in what witnesses say was probably 'the end of the world.' What a shame. The Orb was my favorite go-to place when I wanted to meet someone, but not actually commit to a relationship. Sometimes, you just can't get what you want, can you, Razzmatazz?"

Cindy paused, before covering her face. "I'm sorry," she said, frowning. "I'd forgotten that our sideline reporter, James 'Razzmatazz' Washington, has been arrested for the murder of our cameraman and a lot of other bad stuff. So in case you were wondering, I'm alone. ALL alone! One of my boyfriends is in jail, my other coworker is DEAD. It's JUST ME! DO YOU HEAR ME? JUST ME!"

Cindy threw her notes into the air and stormed off camera. Since she was probably the one who had turned it on to begin with, it remained fixed on the news desk.

*Awkward...*Michael thought.

"Well that's umm...good news, right?" Boris said. "That means that these guys are out of our way now!"

"No, it's NOT good news, Boris," Moe said, shaking his head. "It's stupendous news! Let's celebrate!"

It's not that everyone had forgotten about Ralph's death. In fact, it might have been BECAUSE it was still weighing on them so heavily that they were excited.

Something had finally gone right! The members of the Nervous Sleeve cheered and hugged each other, feeling better than they had in years.

"Oh, I forgot to tell you," Schumer said, laughing as he took some party hats out of the cabinet. "I got another message from our contact!"

"WHAT?" Michael said. "Did they say anything about what happened at the stadium?"

"Or dinner?" Cephas asked, staring at the TV.

"No," Schumer said, placing one of the hats on his head. "It's better!"

"Better than dinner?" Cephas tapped on the screen, hoping it would change.

"They told us..." Schumer said, pausing for dramatic emphasis. "Where Lord Piper's hideout is!"

"NO WAY!" Moe said, grabbing the moose around the neck and rubbing his head. "Where is it?"

"It's at that old monastery right outside of town. I'm not sure how to get there, but I know it's not too far. You know, because it's right outside of town." Schumer smiled.

"That makes so much sense!" Michael said excitedly, grabbing an entire plate of cookies for himself. "That's where Lord Piper grew up! It's where he met the three legged cat! It's where everything began, so of course it's where it's going to end! Why didn't I see it before?"

"I don't know," Crispin said, trying to distract him so she could steal a cookie. "You've been kind of busy."

"That's true," Michael said, moving the plate away from her. "I've been VERY responsible with my studies recently."

"Not so, bro, we left your school," Boris said, shaking his head. "You didn't even take that test your teacher was going to give you. I bet you failed!"

"I would never fail you, Michael!" Grumpy Old Ms. Jones said, giving him an age-appropriate side hug and using her other arm to try to steal a cookie.

"MINE!!!!!!!" Michael yelled, pulling the plate to his chest and shoving the cookies into his mouth.

"It's okay, everybody!" Ruxiben said, entering the room. "I've only got one thing today, but it just so happens to be cookies! Exactly one for each of you, isn't that great?"

"I'm not sure one is going to be enough," Stan said, rubbing his stomach. Now that his vest was off, they could see that he was wearing a striped shirt with a smiling daisy.

"MS JSLSS LDKJ," Michael said, between bites.

"What Michael is trying to say," Crispin smiled as she wiped the crumbs off his shirt, "is that nothing can stop us now! The bad guys are gone! What could possibly go wrong?"

Just then, Miss Dandelion's phone rang. Michael recognized the song from his piano lessons, but he knew it wasn't him because he never practiced. Unless he got paid...

"I'm sorry," Miss Dandelion said, reaching into her purse. "It's probably just a call from my doctor. He was supposed to let me know about the results of..."

She paused, looking down at her phone with a horrified expression. "It can't be," she said. "It's just not possible..."

"What is it?" Boris asked. "Who's calling you?"

"It's Ralph," Miss Dandelion said, putting the phone to her ear.

"H..hhh...hello?" Miss Dandelion asked, her voice shaking almost as much as the hand holding the phone.

"Greetings," said a sinister voice on the other end. It was Ralph's phone, but it was definitely NOT Ralph.

Miss Dandelion gasped.

"Oh, I'M sorry," the voice said impatiently. "Were you expecting someone else?!?"

"I...I...it's just..." Miss Dandelion said. She couldn't finish her sentence. "It's him," she whispered to the others.

Oh good, Ralph! Michael thought happily. *Although I don't know why she seems so worried. That's kind of weird. I guess I DO get kind of nervous when I haven't seen Crispin in a while. Maybe she's just feeling like that?*

"Lord Piper?" Moe asked, looking concerned. "What does he want?"

"It's not Lord Piper, bro!" Boris said, shaking his head. "It's Michael's dad."

He's probably mad about his show...

"Shhh!" Miss Dandelion said, waving for them to stop.

"That's not a very good start to our conversation, Miss Dandelion," the voice said. "If I were you, I would realize I was in no position to be rude."

"What do you want?" Miss Dandelion asked, her voice quivering. "How did you get this phone? What have you done with Ralph?"

But I thought Dad liked Ralph?

"Ralph is fine!" the voice said. "He's safe!"

Miss Dandelion exhaled.

"He's here with me!"

She quickly inhaled again.

"I have a proposition for you and your friends," the voice chuckled. "True to my word, your husband is safe, at least for now. In fact, I have the antidote to

233

everything he's been injected with. One dose of this, and he'll be back to his usual, worthless self. What do you think? Are you ready to make a deal?"

"What's the catch?" Miss Dandelion asked cautiously.

Everyone stared at her, confused. They couldn't hear what was going on, but it sounded like Ralph was alive. They HAD to get him back. They just HAD to!

No matter the cost.

"Always playing hard to get, aren't you?" the voice sneered. "I bet Ralph likes that!"

"Among other things, yes," Miss Dandelion said, holding her stomach.

Why'd she do that? Michael wondered.

"I want the boy, Michael Pumpernickel. You bring him to me, and you can have Ralph AND the antidote. Not a fair trade, but you get what you want and I get what I want. Now isn't that an easy swap?"

Miss Dandelion looked at Michael and shook her head. "We can't do it," she said, sadly.

"But what about Ralph? Don't you want to see him again?" the voice asked. "Or do you want your child to grow up without a father?"

Miss Dandelion gasped, looking around to see if anyone had heard him. They were staring at her in surprise.

"How did you know we're going to have a baby?" she said. "We haven't told anyone!"

WOW! A baby! Michael thought. *That means that I'm going to be an aunt? Cool!*

"Oh, Ralph. Poor, poor Ralph," the voice chuckled. "He may be on his deathbed, but he just can't stop talking about you. He's so worried about your future. Who will take care of you. What will happen to his friends. No thought for his own well being!"

Miss Dandelion started to cry, dropping the phone on the table. Ms. Jones walked over and put an arm around her. Before anyone could stop him, Michael grabbed the phone and put it up to his ear.

"I don't know who you are, or what you want, but let's get one thing straight," Michael said, angrily. "You're NOT going to hurt my brother. He has an awesome wife and an amazing kid on the way. Nothing you can do will change that."

The voice on the other end started to laugh. And laugh. It kind of sounded a little something like this-

"HAHAHAHAHAHA! HACK! HACK! COUGH COUGH COUGH! HACK! Sorry, hairball...HACK!"

Hairball?!?!? Michael thought. "You're the three-legged cat! I thought you were dead!"

"Of course not," the cat said. "I can't die! Or do you *HACK* want me to *HACK* laugh again? Because I will, I don't mind. I'm quite the jolly fellow."

"Listen here, fur ball," Michael said darkly. "You can't have my brother."

"I don't want your brother, truly," the cat said. "You know what I want."

"What a sketchy thing to say to a minor!" Michael glared at the phone.

"YOU KNOW WHAT I MEANT!" the cat shouted. Michael could hear him stomping his three legs in the background.

"Then you can have it," Michael sighed. "If that's the only way we can get Ralph back, we'll give you what you want."

Everyone gasped. Even everyone on the other end of the phone.

"Michael, NO!" Miss Dandelion cried. "Please!"

"I have to," Michael said. "It's my destiny. I always thought I would be the one to defeat Lord Piper, but maybe RALPH is supposed to do it. I mean, the prophecy would have a been a little off, but just a little! He's my brother. If that's true, and I DON'T save Ralph, we've already lost. We all have a part to play. Just let me play mine."

Crispin hugged Michael without saying a word. She didn't have to. Michael knew she supported him no matter what. Even if it meant they'd never be together again.

"Well?" the cat asked. "Is that your final answer?"

Michael took a deep breath. "Yes," he said.

CLICK.

And just like that, the cat was gone. Michael slowly put the phone down on the table and looked at his friends.

These were the people he cared about most in the world. They were the reason he had to give himself away.

"Can I at least, like, go with you bro?" Boris asked.

Michael shook his head. "Like the cat said, it's a clean swap. I don't want to put you in danger."

"Even if you don't let him go, I'M going," Miss Dandelion said, standing up. Michael started to protest, but she stopped him. "And that's FINAL, Michael Pumpernickel."

Michael gasped. In all of his years of taking piano, she had never raised her voice. This was the first time!

"Let them come, Michael," Moe said, holding a party hat awkwardly in his hand. "We can't trust the cat will be fair anyway. He never has been. And plus, they have just as much right to be there as you do. They're family. We all are."

"Moe's right, dear," Mable said, trying to figure out if she should ice the cake she had just baked, or put it away.

"But!" Michael said.

"No buts, Michael," Miss Dandelion said.

Cephas laughed.

"We're coming with you, bro!" Boris grinned.

Michael didn't like it, but he didn't seem to have a choice either. "But what about you guys? I'm not letting all of you come with me. That would be crazy! If we fail, the Sleeve has to live on!"

"We're not coming with you," Crispin said, shaking her head. "What I mean is...we can't. We've got a LOT to do before you come back. ALL of you."

"That's right," Grumpy Old Ms. Jones said, putting her hand on Crispin's shoulder. "I was talking with Crispin, and she's agreed to go back to the school with me."

"The school?!?" Michael said. "But why?"

"Why?" Ms. Jones asked, chuckling. "To take back my classroom, of course!" She smiled, a look of determination on her face. Michael laughed. The Harrington Twin had no idea what was coming for him.

Bad times. VERY bad times...

"That's not all," Moe said. "While you guys are away, the rest of us can come up with a plan of attack for the monastery. By the time you get back, we'll be ready to go. Rendezvous at the Dandy Cardinal. We'll be set after that!"

Michael was silent, staring at the ground. The members of the Nervous Sleeve held their breath (or breaths?), unsure of how he would react. They needed more than just his help to get their plan off the ground. They needed his support.

"I like it," Michael said. "This just might be crazy enough to work!"

"Then what are we waiting for?" Moe asked. "Let's go!"

"I can't believe this place is still here!" Michael said, shaking his head as they walked up to the warehouse.

"I know!" Miss Dandelion frowned. "We saw it fall down, didn't we?"

"I don't know, like, I was dead when that happened I think," Boris said, shrugging. "So I didn't see it but..."

"You weren't ACTUALLY dead, Boris," Michael laughed.

"Really?!? Man, that explains SO MUCH!!!!" Boris said, shocked.

"I don't know what my sister sees in you," Miss Dandelion smiled, nudging the bass player in the ribs.

"OW! I don't either, but I don't want to ask like just in case," Boris said, a look of concern on his face. "You know? Cause that could be really bad."

"Hey, I'm really tired, do you guys want a break?" Michael asked. He sat down on the curb and took out a pack of Choco Squares.

"I'm always on break," Boris said, joining him.

They'd had to walk to the warehouse because the cab company shut down when Razzmatazz went on the run. Kind of a bummer, but it just gave Michael the excuse to eat more, which he was totally fine with.

"We should probably go on in and save Ralph," Miss Dandelion said, pacing back and forth. "We don't want to keep the cat waiting."

"But we don't want to be hungry either!" Michael said. "That might have a negative effect on our 'saving' performance! Ralph wouldn't want that."

"He's got a point," Boris said, reaching for the Choco Squares.

"NO!" Michael yelled, spitting crumbs everywhere.

"I think we should go on inside," the bass player scowled, no longer interested in eating. "What's the plan?"

Michael looked at Miss Dandelion.

"Don't look at me, Michael, YOU'RE the leader. You were going to come alone, remember? What were you planning on doing?" she asked.

"I don't really know," Michael said, shrugging. "I was hoping to figure something out on the way over, but I didn't do too much thinking because we were singing the whole time."

"And rapping," Boris added.

"Don't get me wrong," Michael said, smiling. "I LOVE singing, AND I'm really good at it, but I'm NOT good at doing two things at once."

"Besides talking and eating," Miss Dandelion sighed, looking longingly at the door.

"Hey wait, I've got it!" Michael said, standing up, triumphantly. "Follow me."

"That's it?!?" Miss Dandelion asked. "You're not going to tell us the plan?"

"If I told you the plan it would go against the plan," Michael said like it was obvious.

"I totally get that," Boris said, nodding. "Let's go."

Miss Dandelion groaned and followed them into the warehouse. Remembering where he had been kidnapped, Michael walked confidently to the door that led to the cat's lab. He paused, turning around.

"Just follow my lead," he said. He was hoping that he sounded WAYYYYYYYY more confident than he felt.

They both nodded. Michael took a deep breath and opened the door.

"You're late!" the cat snarled, walking toward them. "And you didn't come alone!"

"Of course I didn't come alone, you didn't ask me to," Michael said angrily. He hated cats. Especially THIS cat. They made him sneeze and he didn't like that.

"I didn't? Well I MEANT to," the cat frowned, glaring at them. "That should count for something, don't you think?"

"Umm..." Michael said, looking at the others.

"WELL?!?!?!?!" the cat yelled.

"GROANNNNNN MOANNNNNNNNN GROAN GROAN GROANNNNNN...."

Ralph! Michael thought, looking around.

His brother, still a monster, was heavily sedated and strapped to a table. But there were two other people in the room too. Two people he didn't expect!

"I see you've noticed my other guests," the cat chuckled, motioning for the turtle to hand him a syringe. "I didn't realize I was popular enough for the police chief to pay me a visit, but then again, I'm so modest!"

"POLICE CHIEF EARL GREY?" Michael gasped.

Yes, Michael. That's what he just said. Pay attention. Come on, this is YOUR book.

He's from the news! Michael thought. *I didn't know he was a REAL police chief! Who's the other guy? Is that Chad from the prison? What is HE doing here?!?!?*

"Michael, what's your plan?" Miss Dandelion asked, looking irritated as the Cardinal cardinal walked behind her with a crowbar. "Was it to just walk in here unarmed and figure something out later because you're hungry?"

Guilty, Michael thought.

Miss Dandelion sighed.

"Ummm...well, it seemed like a good idea in my head," Michael shrugged. "LAST time, we had the element of surprise. I thought if we did the complete opposite THIS TIME, they wouldn't be expecting it. Plus, I was hungry."

"I wasn't expecting it!" Boris said.

"Me neither," Miss Dandelion groaned.

(Me neither!)

"It wouldn't have mattered," the cat said, shaking his head. "You promised me Michael. He's all I want."

"Okay, I'm not really that into you," Michael said, backing up. He bumped into the Cardinal who waved the crowbar menacingly.

"Let me show you how the serum works," the cat said, walking over to the table with the police chief. "Maybe then you can see what I'm trying to accomplish."

Earl Grey squirmed nervously.

"You see, our friend came to find me after the Razzmatazz 'incident' became national news," the cat said. "I have you to thank for that, Boris. I guess we didn't do a good enough job of killing you."

"No sir!" the bass player said, smiling. "But then again, it's hard to kill someone who's..."

"A champion, I know," the cat said, waving his hand.

"You know my catchphrase?" Boris gasped. "Are you trying to steal it?"

"No, you're predictable," the cat said dismissively.

Boris frowned.

"The point is, I'm going to inject Mr. Grey, here, using the same thing I injected your brother with, Michael," the cat continued. "To make it more fun, I'm going to use SIX syringes, chosen at random from my collection. Then I will apply the serum showing how effective it can be."

The cat motioned to a surprisingly organized shelf of vials of different colors, shapes and sizes. It was beautiful in its own way.

"This is horrible, we need to DO SOMETHING!" Miss Dandelion gasped.

Agreed, but I'm strangely fascinated, Michael thought, inching forward to get a better look.

"CAW! CAW! CAW!" the Cardinal said, shaking his head. He hadn't been able to find another necklace, so he was stuck talking like a crow. Or, a cardinal, but they probably sound the same.

"Don't talk to us like that, bro!" Boris said, sticking out his tongue.

The cat smiled. "Focus everyone, this is important."

With the angry turtle's assistance, the cat shoved an entire board of needles into the police chief's back. The policeman screamed in terror, transforming before their eyes.

"Wow, that looks like Ralph!" Michael said as Earl Grey began to grow fur. *Which one IS he? I guess I've never paid much attention to what my brother looks like...*

"Now, as promised, the serum!" the cat said, taking a to-go box out from under the table with a flourish. He removed a piece of decadent looking chocolate cake and started to feed it to the police chief with what looked like a spork.

You have to admit, he's got style. I hope he has enough for everybody!

"Wait, the serum is cake?" Miss Dandelion asked.

"Of course it is," the cat said. "I've found that chocolate can cure anything."

So true. So, very true...

Police Chief Earl Grey finished his transformation and immediately fainted. Michael was kind of disappointed at how quickly the whole thing had gone down.

"And now, for the main event," the cat laughed. "It's time, Michael."

"But you haven't cured Ralph!" Michael frowned, crossing his arms. He was trying to stall so he could figure out how to get some cake. "At least let me say goodbye!"

The cat looked like he was going to explode with anger, but quickly returned to his usual 'charming' self. "Of course, Michael. Anything for you."

Michael rushed over and knelt down beside his brother. He glanced at the cat and started to loosen Ralph's chains. *I should break him out if I'm going to eat his cake...*

"What are you doing?" the cat snapped."You're not talking! How is that 'saying' goodbye in the literal sense?"

"It's umm...it's not," Michael said, putting his hands in the air and hoping he'd done enough. "Ralph and I have a deep psychological connection. He can read minds."

"He CAN?!?!?!" Boris asked, amazed.

"No, he CAN'T," Miss Dandelion groaned.

"Alright, alright. Enough is enough!" the cat said angrily. Keeping one eye on the others, he walked toward Michael and grabbed him by the collar. "I've got a table with your name on it! And no, I actually don't. It's an expression. Don't say it because I know you're thinking it."

Drat!

RRRRRRRRRRRRRRRRRRRRRIP!!!!!!

Suddenly, the collar of Michael's favorite shirt split open. "Blast!" the cat said. He had gone TOO FAR.

"NOT MY FAVORITE SHIRT!!!!" Michael yelled, punching the abbot. The cat fell to the ground, unconscious. *Wow!* Michael thought, looking at his hand, confused.

It was exactly the distraction that they needed! Seeing an opportunity, Boris snatched the crow bar from the Cardinal and started beating everything he saw.

"CAW CAW CAW!" the Cardinal screeched urgently, pointing at Michael's brother.

"Why don't you do something about it yourself!" the angry turtle snapped, as he tried to drag the cat to safety.

The cardinal's eyes grew wide as a shadow came over them.

"He's right behind me, isn't he?" the turtle frowned, shaking his head. "I knew we shouldn't have gotten those chains at the Super Duper Save Clearance Sale..."

Suddenly, Ralph lifted the turtle into the air and threw him across the room. He landed against the far wall with a crack and collapsed to the ground.

"WE HAVE TO GET RALPH SOME CAKE!" Miss Dandelion cried.

"Don't worry, I'LL protect you!" Boris said, swinging the crowbar in circles. "I can beat this dude up!"

"Don't hurt him, SAVE HIM!" Miss Dandelion screamed. Ralph was getting closer.

"Oh, okay," Boris said, scratching his head. "Where's the cake?"

251

"Found it!" Michael said, pulling a to-go box out from under the table. "Here!"

He tossed it to the bass player, but it was intercepted by the Cardinal in midair.

"CAW CAW CAW!" the Cardinal said, dropping the box of cake into the trash.

"WHAT ARE YOU DOING?" Miss Dandelion screamed. "What a waste of chocolate..."

"He can't tell us, he only talks like a bird!" Boris said, looking at Michael desperately. "Michael, what do we do? We can't feed Ralph the cake now! That's gross!"

Michael looked up guiltily, chocolate cake all over his face. He'd eaten the last piece because he'd thought they only needed one. Now their last hope was on its way down his stomach!

"Dern fern!" he yelled, angrily.

"Michael, WHAT DID YOU DO?!?!?" Miss Dandelion screamed.

It's not about what I ALREADY did, but about what I'm GOING to do, Michael thought, suddenly having an idea. *It's not a great idea, but it's an idea. Oh goodness, I hope this works!*

"Hey, UGLY!" he yelled, jumping up and down. Ralph turned to face him and roared, shaking the foundation.

"Bro, what's going on?" Boris whispered, trying to do the opposite of what Michael was doing. He didn't want ANY attention.

"That's right!" Michael yelled, ignoring the bass player and waving his arms. "Why don't you come on over here? I'm tired of you shedding on all of my stuff!"

Ralph growled, walking towards Michael.

"MICHAEL!" Miss Dandelion yelled. "STOP!"

"It's okay, guys," Michael said, his voice shaking. "It's all part of the plan."

"We have a plan now?" Boris asked.

Michael covered his face as Ralph reached down and grabbed him. *This is nuts!* he thought, closing his eyes.

And then Ralph swallowed him whole.

Yeah, you read that right. Michael just got eaten by his brother! So, common sense would say that the book is probably over. WRONG. Guess again.

.....

Have you guessed? If not, what's taking so long?!?!?!

.....

Okay, I'm telling you anyway. Michael's alive! Sorry. Wait, no! I'm NOT sorry! Why in the world would you want our hero to be dead? Seriously, you're SICK.

SICK.

The bad news is you took so long guessing, that we actually missed the most exciting part. Because Michael had eaten chocolate cake and was COVERED in chocolate cake, Ralph turned back into a human and everybody lived.

I know that doesn't make a ton of sense, but this IS a book. Don't believe me? Check it out-

"I don't think I'll EVER do that again," Michael coughed, looking at his brother.

"Yeah, me neither," Ralph chuckled. He was standing next to Miss Dandelion with his hand around her shoulders. "So you know, like, what happened? I know I was a monster and all, but I got kind of lost around the time I ate you."

"Me too," Michael frowned. "It was pretty dark in there. And sticky."

"I don't remember anything," Boris shrugged. "I think I spaced out or something. When I woke up, Ralph was here. Then, Michael WASN'T here. Then, Michael WAS here! It gave me a killer headache."

"We're just doing our duty, Mr. Frankfurter," Police Chief Earl Grey said, smiling. The three-legged cat and his associates were chained up in the other room.

"Giving people headaches?" Boris asked. "Is that what my tax dollars go to? What kind of messed up city IS this?"

"You don't pay taxes, Boris, you're a freeloader," Miss Dandelion sighed.

The police chief smiled as he dug into a mangled-looking box of doughnuts. "What? They were in my pocket," he frowned, noticing everyone staring at him.

"I wasn't going to say anything," Michael said, saying something anyway. "I can appreciate foods of all shapes and sizes."

"Can I have one, boss?" Chad in Security asked. "We used to get them at the Prison, and I have to say I really regret not working there for that very reason."

"No problem," the police chief said, picking a particularly messy jelly filled doughnut out of the box and handing it to Chad.

The security guard paused, frowning. "Wait a second..where did it go?!?"

Michael smiled proudly, jelly all over his face.

"You've got an incredible gift, son," Earl Grey laughed, turning to Michael.

"What about my doughnut?" Chad asked.

"Well, don't get greedy, you only get one!" the police chief frowned, shaking his head. "Now, Mr. Pumpernickel. Either of you. What happened here."

"Even though we just got done telling you we don't really know," Michael shrugged, "I'm going to make it all up and mix in the parts that are actually real."

"Sounds good to me," Earl Grey said. He took out a pad of paper and began to scribble on it, even before Michael had started talking. "Go ahead," he nodded.

So Michael explained everything that had been going on. Even the things that the police chief probably didn't need to know like details about his love life and what color socks he was wearing. When he was done talking, Earl Grey did NOT look happy.

"I can't believe so much corruption has been going on under our noses, Chad," he said, smoothing his mustache and frowning. "This is all your fault!"

"But I just started working here!" Chad said, angrily. "I quit my other job because it was too stressful!"

"Not that, Chad!" the police chief said, shaking his head. "I KNOW you didn't cause the infiltration of our government by talking animal spies. It's your fault that I just got jelly on my mustache! If you hadn't asked me to share with you, I wouldn't have it all over my face!"

Chad stared at him in disbelief. "I didn't even get a doughnut," he said, gritting his teeth.

"I got a doughnut AND cake!" Michael smiled.

"Unbelievable," Chad sighed.

"So can you really take our grandpa off death row?" Ralph asked, changing the subject. "You know, since it was Lord Piper who was behind all of that bad stuff?"

"Oh, absolutely, son!" the police chief chuckled. "It would be my pleasure! After all, it's a cause to celebrate!" He looked at the empty box of doughnuts and threw it to the ground. "And celebrations mean more doughnuts!"

Everyone stood around awkwardly.

"Well, we're off!" the police chief said abruptly. "Chad and I have a LOT of work ahead of us. We have to take these animals down to the station and then go free your grandfather!"

"Cool," Michael said. "Party at your place later?"

The police chief furrowed his brow and shook his head. "No, I think I want all of the doughnuts to myself, thank you."

SOCKS! First, no one comes to MY party! And then I can't come to someone else's?

"Count me in!" Boris said, giving the police chief a thumbs up. "Wait," he said, pausing. "You just said 'no,' didn't you? Man!" The bass player hung his head.

"Goodbye Pumpernickels, Miss Dandelion and that other guy!" Police Chief Earl Grey said as he walked to where the abbot and his followers were being held. Chad was close behind. "I'll see you at the doughnut shop!"

"Oh boy, doughnuts!" Michael said, smiling.

"We can't go eat doughnuts," Miss Dandelion said, shaking her head. "We have to go meet the others."

"Hmmm..." Michael thought, trying to figure out how to lose the group. "Never mind, let's do it." He had remembered something even better than doughnuts.

Crispin!

"Wow! This is like a date!" Michael said, holding Crispin's hand and gazing into her eyes. "It totally makes up for the one that we were going to have earlier when I went out with Ralph instead."

"That wasn't a date," Ralph said, frowning. "You're my brother."

"I know!" Michael said. "Weird."

"Hey, so what did you guys find out?" Miss Dandelion asked as the owner of The Dandy Cardinal brought them a full tray of food and drinks. He still hadn't forgotten about the business they had given him a few years back during the 'Exploding Flyer Incident.' Things just hadn't been the same.

Aha! Doughnuts! Michael thought, grabbing the entire basket. *I wonder if this place has free refills? That's MY kind of doughnut slash coffee shop.*

"We got my classroom back!" Grumpy Old Ms. Jones said, proudly. She had a fresh cut on her forehead that looked pretty brutal.

"Wait. Whoa. What happened to your face?" Boris asked, looking up. He was drawing a picture of a seahorse on the moon. "Has that always been there?"

"No, dear," Ms. Jones laughed. "I just got it, actually. It's still pretty fresh." Blood dripped down onto Boris' drawing. (Yeah, that's pretty fresh!)

The bass player gasped, clutching his heart. "My picture!" he frowned. "Wait a second...wicked! We make a good 'art' team!" He seemed pretty pleased with himself.

"Are you okay, Margaret?" Miss Dandelion asked, handing her sister a napkin. "Is she okay?" she said, turning to Crispin.

"She's fine," Crispin laughed. "It was actually easier than we thought! When we got there, we expected to find one of the Harrington Twins. We did, but just not the one we thought we would."

"Wait, how many of them are there?" Michael asked, confused. "Because I already killed one of them and the other one WAS my teacher. Are you saying there are three twins?"

"You killed someone?" Ms. Jones asked, horrified.

"Sort of," Michael frowned. New doughnuts hadn't magically appeared in his basket yet. *What kind of place IS this? The disappointment keeps growing...*

"Apparently, you didn't do a very good job," Crispin laughed. "There ARE only two twins (which is pretty typical), but it wasn't our teacher we saw. It was Alonzo, your bodyguard."

"He had a name?" Michael gasped.

"Didn't you, like, stab him?" Boris asked, smearing blood across the seahorse's face.

"You stabbed someone?!?" Ms. Jones, gasped.

"Sort of," Michael shrugged. "I can't believe he lived. But then again, I can't believe his name is Alonzo."

"Anyway," Crispin said. "We called the cops because he was trespassing, and after a short scuffle, Police Chief Earl Grey arrived and arrested him. Can you believe he's an actual cop? I thought he was just a guy on TV!"

"ME TOO!!!" Michael said, smiling at her.

"So that's one twin down, that's great!" Ralph said, excitedly. "We can add him to the list of people we don't have to worry about anymore- Jerry, Goodburn, Doogie, Goddard, Razzmatazz, Dexterum Dei. And I mean it, let's make a list because there's too many characters in this story. But where's the other twin?"

"Does he look like his brother?" Boris asked, squinting at something behind them.

"They're twins," Michael said, rolling his eyes. "That means all three of them look the same."

"That doesn't necessarily follow," Ms. Jones said. "As your teacher, I should tell you that..."

"Then that might be him!" Boris yelled, pointing to someone in the corner.

The Twin turned and looked in their direction. They quickly ducked below the table.

(I ducked as well. You can never be too careful...)

"Michael, why aren't you wearing any shoes?" Miss Dandelion asked, looking at Michael's bare feet.

Michael looked down, his eyes wide. "I have no idea," he said. *I hope I'm not naked by the time I get home! That would be a tad breezy.*

"Is it safe to look up?" Ralph whispered.

"I'm looking up now and all I can see is the table," Boris said. "It is nice though. Wow, is that mahogany?"

"Let's try it," Crispin shrugged.

They all sat up and looked at the corner apprehensively. The Twin must not have recognized them because he hadn't moved. That was pretty lucky.

"Peanuts, that was close!" Michael sighed, wiping the sweat off his forehead. "Now what?"

"We listen in and lay low!" Ralph said. "Look!"

While they were under the table, Dapply had walked in! He was busy making himself comfortable at the Twin's table. The Twin didn't look comfortable though. He kept glancing at the door and fidgeting with his hair.

"I don't know why you're so upset, Gerald," Dapply snapped, tying a napkin around his neck. "Everything is going according to plan."

"According to plan?" the Twin said, angrily. "Half of Lord Piper's minions are dead, or worse...in jail!"

"That's nothing to get worked up over," Dapply scoffed, trying to get the owner's attention. "Especially since Lord Piper's tests are complete. The new necklace is unstoppable!"

"But we need numbers, Dapply! NUMBERS!"

"Oh, we've got that," Dapply chuckled. "HEY YOU!!!" he yelled, slamming his fist on the table. "WHAT'S IT TAKE TO GET CRABS OVER HERE?!?"

The owner quickly walked over, looking flustered. "Sir, this is a coffee shop. We don't serve crabs."

"Then what DO you serve?" Dapply snapped.

"Mostly coffee," the owner shrugged, waving his hand across the room to show Dapply what the other customers had ordered.

The organist was about to look in their direction when Police Chief Earl Grey walked up, blocking his view.

"How are you so many places at once?" Ralph asked, astonished.

"To tell you the truth, I think it's the sugar," Earl Grey said, shrugging. "Anyway, I'm glad you're here. I wanted to let you know that your grandpa has been cleared of all charges! He's been moved off of death row effective immediately!"

Michael and Ralph sighed in relief.

"We've also been able to identify a few double agents in the department because of Jerry Mudwater's plea deal. Don't worry," he said reassuringly. "We haven't let him go. It was for a reduced sentence."

I'm so relieved, Michael thought.

"Well, that's that," the police chief said brightly. "What does this place serve anyway?"

"Mostly coffee," Ralph said. "I wouldn't ask for anything else though. It doesn't go over well." He pointed to the corner where Dapply and the owner were still fighting.

"I WANT CRABS! I WANT CRABS! I WANT CRABS! I WANT CRABS! I WANT CRABS! I WANT CRABS! I WANT CRABS! I WANT CRABS! I WANT CRABS! I WANT CRABS! I WANT CRABS! I WANT CRABS!"

"Is that Dapply Clemmons?" the police chief asked. "There's an outstanding warrant for his arrest! And the other guy looks like the guy I just took in an hour ago! Are they twins? I've got to call in backup!"

Earl Grey took out his cell phone and held it up to his ear. "Yes, we need reinforcements," he said. "What? Doughnuts? Yes, we need those too. Oh," he frowned. "This is the doughnut shop? That explains it, yes. Yes. No. Delivery, yes. Chocolate. Okay," he sighed, putting his phone on the table. "We're good to go."

"But I thought you were getting backup?" Crispin asked, confused.

"I did get backup," the police chief said, smiling. "FOOD! It turns out I have the doughnut shop on speed dial, NOT my precinct. It was a happy coincidence. But no matter. I made Chad wait by the door, so he's here too."

Michael looked over and saw Chad sitting on the ground by the register.

"Hey, Chad! Get over here!" the police chief yelled.

Chad stood up, looking relieved. "My legs were starting to cramp down there," he said. "What's up, boss?"

"Go arrest those guys," Earl Grey said, waving his hand and sitting down at the table with Michael and the others.

"Alone?!?" Chad asked, horrified.

"Certainly not!" the police chief chuckled. "You can ask anyone you want, you're a policeman, after all! A champion of the common man! A public servant! They HAVE to do what you say! I've used that line to confiscate quite a few boxes of doughnuts over the years."

"Will you help me then?" Chad squealed as a chair flew over his head and crashed through the window.

"No, I said ask someone," the police chief said. "Ah...oh, wait. I see your point. Okay."

It didn't take long for the two of them to subdue Dapply. He'd been so distracted by his fight with the owner he hadn't seen them coming. The twin was even easier to arrest. He turned himself in!

"You're too late," Dapply sneered, as they passed Michael's table. "Lord Piper can't be stopped!" The villain's laughter could be heard through the broken window as the police car pulled away.

"'Lord Piper cannot be stopped!'" Boris chuckled, mocking the organist. "I never liked that guy anyway. Minotaur is a terrible band."

"I thought you liked Minotaur, dear?" Grumpy Old Ms. Jones asked, confused.

"Shhhhh..." Boris whispered, looking embarrassed.

"So add two MORE to our list!" Ralph said excitedly. "Lord Piper has no one left!"

"That's not exactly true," Michael said, worriedly. "He's still got Chet, Grohill, Todd, Tugley. That mystery necklace. Wow, there really are a lot of characters..."

"But you can't worry about that, Michael!" Crispin said brightly. "This is a BIG day! This is a HUGE victory for the Nervous Sleeve!"

Michael wasn't convinced, but he didn't stop them from celebrating. He just had a feeling that before it was all over, something unexpected was going to happen, for better, or for worse.

MOO! MOO! MOO! MOO! MOO! MOO! MOO!

Michael jumped in his seat.

"Oh, sorry guys!" Boris said. "That's my cell."

Who would be calling at a time like this? Michael wondered. He hoped it wasn't something bad, or unexpected. You know, for better, or for worse.

It was. Well, something unexpected. It wasn't bad. It was actually really good!

"It's Moe!" Boris said, switching on speaker phone so the others could listen in. "What's up, bro?"

"Good news," Moe said, his voice full of excitement. "You won't believe who's here! And you'll never guess...he knows how to find the monastery!"

Michael prepared himself. After all, their mission had been a complete success. Obviously, everybody was going to throw them a party when they got back to Hungry Woody's. He paused before opening the door to the kitchen, trying to guess what kind of cake they'd have.

Chocolate? Marshmallow? Peanut butter?

"Michael, get out of the way," Ralph said, pushing him to the side. "Alice needs to sit down and rest. Plus, you're just being annoying." He opened the door and Michael caught a glimpse of the room.

Hmm...I don't see any cake! he thought. *Maybe it's too big for the kitchen and it's outside? I hope not though because it's raining. I had wet cake once and it was weird because I couldn't use a fork. The fork is the best part!*

"I know, I didn't see any cake either," Crispin said, frowning. "But on the bright side, aren't you still full from all those doughnuts? You probably didn't have room anyway. You wouldn't have enjoyed it."

"No, I did," Michael said, his stomach rumbling.

Crispin laughed.

They walked into the kitchen and it was about as opposite of a party as you can get. Everyone was sitting down and facing a large map of Some Town. They were listening to someone Michael hadn't seen in a long time. A VERY long time. Like, almost two whole books.

It was the mysterious frog!

"WHAT IS HE DOING HERE?" Michael yelled, backing up.

The last time he'd seen that guy really bad things had happened. He was already pretty broken up about no cake, so he didn't want anything else to ruin his day.

Plus, frogs are scary. They make startling movements. I don't think I can handle that right now.

"Michael! Crispin! Thanks for joining us!" the frog said, motioning to two seats in the front. "We were just talking about how we're going to defeat Lord Piper."

"But like...what are you doing here?" Michael asked, sitting down in the back instead. "You're creepy. And weird. I thought you just wrote stuff down."

The frog smiled. "I can see how it would be hard for you to understand my line of work. It's a solitary life."

"I mean, I like to write things too from time to time," Michael said, rolling his eyes. "My diary is already halfway full, and I got it when I turned seven! That means, if I don't slow down, I only have six more years to live."

"That's not how that works," the frog said.

Oh, good. I had started to write really small and it was making my hand cramp...

"Michael, this is Orion," Moe said, standing up and putting his arm around the frog. "He's not just the narrator of the story, he's much more important than that."

(Thanks!)

"We were doing some research about the town and put the pieces together. It just clicked! It all made sense." Moe grinned and the others nodded.

"What made sense?" Crispin asked.

"Orion is the third founder of Burlwood Forest Village!" Cephas said excitedly. "He's the monk who left Three Paws Hall with Tugley and Lord Piper."

"But wait..." Michael said, scratching his head. "If that's true, where have you been all these years? Why didn't anybody, like, know this before?"

"Well, I have been here, Michael," the frog said sadly. "But just as people tend to forget history, they also forget those who make it. You saw how I slipped by unnoticed at the Festival of the Trees."

"That's probably just because of that purple smoke though," Michael said. "Everybody was umm...distracted."

"It's not just that," the frog said, hanging his head. "I was a coward from the start. Even though I was brave enough to stand up to my own order, when it came to Lord Piper, I'm afraid I did a poor job. When I couldn't face that reality, I drifted into the shadows. It was easier that way."

"But you're a hero!" Michael said, looking around at the others. "You were the one who stood up for Lord Piper when no one else would! When he was good and stuff."

"That's the thing," Orion said. "I think he still is."

"WHAT ARE YOU TALKING ABOUT?!?" Ralph shouted, pointing a finger at the frog. "Lord Piper ruined my life! He's ruined all of our lives!"

"He broke up my band!" Boris said angrily.

"YOU'RE NOT IN A BAND!!!" everyone yelled.

The bass player blushed and sunk down in his seat.

"Orion's right," Moe said. "No one is too far from saving. If my time in jail taught me anything, I know the power of redemption and forgiveness."

"But how can you say that?!?" Miss Dandelion asked. "He's done so much evil!"

"Yes, he has," Orion said. "But haven't we all? Wasn't it just as evil for me to sit around and do nothing? I saw the hurt he caused! I saw the pain! But I just watched. Even when I was able to do more."

"None of us are perfect," Mable said, beginning to cry. "I thought that Lord Piper could help me save the orphanage."

"And I thought he could, like, help my band get big," Boris said. No one corrected him.

"It wasn't until I talked with members of the Sleeve, that I realized how wrong I'd been," the frog said.

"But I still don't get it," Crispin frowned, shaking her head. "How did they find you?"

"Funny story, actually," Schumer chuckled, looking at Stan.

Michael whirled around. He hadn't seen the moose sitting behind him! *Sketch...I'm in the back row too, how did he DO that?!?*

"After we figured out the frog was the narrator, the narrator was Orion and Orion was the third founder, we just kind of said something hoping he would hear us," Stan shrugged.

"Naturally, I did," Orion said, smiling. "But I was scared, so I didn't say anything back."

"That's when we tried to bribe him with a fresh batch of Stan's cookies," Moe said. "As you know, they're pretty hard to resist."

"Are there any left?!?" Michael asked, excitedly.

"But Orion refused," Moe continued, ignoring him.

"What?" Michael gasped. "How can you do that?"

"I'm watching my weight," the frog shrugged. "I'm also scared of cookies, I had a bad experience."

"How can you have a bad experience with cookies?" Ms. Jones asked, confused.

"This one time, I bought a bag that was supposed to be Mr. Magnificent's Triple Dipple Fudge Rounds, but it ended up having nuts in it," the frog sighed. "It was nasty."

"I'd say!" Michael said. "But your first mistake was going with Mr. Magnificent over Mr. Sugar! That guy will rip you off any chance he gets!"

"It just so happened that Ruxiben walked in right when we were about to give up," Moe said. "And as always, he had..."

"Precisely what you needed!" the bear said, walking into the room. He was noisily eating his hat again, and this time, it looked like it was made of jam.

"What was it?" Crispin asked.

"He had a blue and white striped shirt with a green collar!" Moe said, holding it up.

"But that's MY shirt!" Michael said, looking down at himself, frantically. "That's my FAVORITE shirt! You can't have it! It's MINE!"

"Yours is green and white with a BLUE collar!" Cephas said to everyone's surprise.

"Aren't you blind?" Mable asked, shaking her head.

"But what does that shirt have to do with anything?" Michael asked. "I mean, whoever owns it has pretty good taste, but I don't get why it's important."

"It's important because it's LORD PIPER'S favorite shirt!" Moe said triumphantly.

"WHAT?!?" Michael gasped, starting to choke. COUGH! COUGH! COUGH! COUGH! COUGH! COUGH! COUGH! COUGH! COUGH! COUGH! COUGH! COUGH! COUGH! COUGH! COUGH!

"Sorry," he said, regaining his composure. "I just thought you said Lord Piper had a similar favorite shirt to me. That's all."

"He does," the frog said, nodding.

"NOOOOOOOOOOOOOOOOOOOOOOOO!!!!!!!!!!"

"Michael, it's alright!" Orion said, motioning for Moe to put the shirt down, preferably out of sight. "It's because of that shirt that I'm here! When Ruxiben gave it to Moe, it reminded me of the animal Lord Piper HAD been. It reminded me of who he COULD be. I know he's done bad things, but all I could think about is the scared troublemaker I stood up for all those years ago. I know he's still inside there somewhere, and I think you know that too. Remember your talk with him at the Parade of Animals?"

"Wait...how did you know about that?" Michael asked, confused. "Oh wait, you're the narrator. That's weird."

"You see what I mean?" Orion asked. "Nothing is as white and black as we make it. Everyone has a reason for what they do, whether it's good or bad. Sometimes, we think we're doing the right thing when we're not."

"But Lord Piper can't possibly think he's doing the right thing!" Miss Dandelion said angrily. "After all he's done to Ralph! After all he's done to Michael!"

This time, it was Michael's turn to surprise everybody. "Lord Piper hasn't been perfect, Miss Dandelion. Far from it. But in the same situation, I can't say that I wouldn't have done the same thing. Orion is right. We have to learn to forgive."

"So we're not going to, like, storm the monastery?" Boris asked, disappointed.

"That's not really the plan, no," Moe said, shaking his head. "Sorry."

"Awww man!!!!!!" Boris said, crossing his arms.

"But that brings up a good point," Ralph said, sitting up in his chair. "Even though we don't want to attack Lord Piper, which I don't necessarily agree with, what if he attacks US? We can't just stand there and let him do it."

"Ralph's right," Grumpy Old Ms. Jones said. "I'm not just walking in there without a plan. What if my nails get chipped?"

"Don't worry," Michael smiled. "I have a plan."

Miss Dandelion groaned. "It's not like your LAST plan, is it? The one where you didn't have a plan, but were just really hungry?"

"Hey, that plan worked!" Michael said defiantly. "Ralph's here, isn't he?"

Michael's brother shrugged. "You can't argue with the results, Alice."

"But that was just blind luck!" Miss Dandelion snapped. "This is Lord Piper we're talking about! We can't take any chances!"

"What if my heel breaks?" Ms. Jones frowned.

"What if he tricks me again?" Mable said, crying.

"What if he invites me to HIS band?" Boris asked.

"What if we just trusted each other?" Moe sighed, throwing his hands up in the air.

The room became silent. Michael didn't have the greatest track record with plans, but no one else had one either. They'd seen the disastrous consequences of inaction before.

"We can't wait to go to the monastery," Orion said. "Even though I think Lord Piper can be saved, I fear he's quickly slipping to a place he can't come back from. Michael, please tell us what we can do."

Michael looked at Crispin and smiled. She always made him feel confident. He slowly walked to the front of the room and took a deep breath, staring at the blue and white striped shirt with the green collar. *Lord Piper was right. We DO have more in common than I thought...*

Michael gazed out at his friends and knew they were going to succeed. Not because of HIS plan, or even anything HE would do, but because they were together. They were family.

"Okay, here's my plan," he said.

This is the part of the story where I wish I could tell you more, I really do. But I mean...that would ruin everything, right? Not cool.

So when we're talking and we say something like 'he,' 'she,' or 'them,' just roll with it. You'll find out soon enough. The end is near! No, not the end of the world. The end of the book!

"Do you think they'll get there in time?" Michael frowned, looking down at the map.

They'd taken the giant wall-sized one from Hungry Woody's so they wouldn't get lost. Unfortunately, they couldn't get it out of the frame. And really unfortunately, it was heavy. SUPER HEAVY.

"I think if we don't get there soon, I'm going to break or something," Boris said, his voice straining under the weight of the map.

"I told you, I can help if you want me to?" Schumer asked, hopefully.

"NOO!!!!!" Boris yelled, almost bumping into Stan.

The moose frowned. "I'm not THAT clumsy."

"Of course, not," Stan grunted.

"Stop moving, you need to hold the map still," Michael snapped. He'd come up with a dynamite plan, but it was only awesome if it worked. Now that it was actually happening, he was starting to have his doubts.

"But we have to move! We're supposed to be walking right now," Stan groaned, starting to sweat.

"I don't know why you're complaining, bro!" Boris grunted. "This isn't hard...when you're a champion." The bass player sighed. He didn't have a free hand to run through his close cropped hair!

"It's alright, Michael," Orion said, shaking his head. "I know how to find the monastery. It's quite close to here, actually. It's right by your house!"

"Really?" Michael asked, astounded. "How come I haven't seen it before?"

"Probably because you haven't been looking for it," the frog shrugged.

So wise, yet so....not helpful, Michael thought. "If you know where it is, why did you tell Boris and Stan to carry the map?"

Orion chuckled. "I didn't. They decided that all on their own!"

Michael smiled.

"But I'm not as clever as you think," the frog continued. "The main reason I know where the monastery is located is because it's right here." He pointed to a bright red star on the map labeled 'THREE PAWS HALL.'

"Oh," Michael said. "Ohhhhhhh. I'd never thought about that. It seemed too obvious."

"Sometimes, the very thing we're looking for is right in front of us," Orion chuckled, nodding at Crispin. "She's special, Michael."

"I know you're talking about me," Crispin said. "I hope it's only good things."

"So far," Michael said, winking. *Wait...*

"Bros, can we talk about how heavy this map is?" Boris asked. "Where ARE we?"

"You have the map, dear," Grumpy Old Ms. Jones said. "You tell us!"

"I can't read!" Boris frowned.

"Technically, you don't have to know how to read to understand a map," Stan said. "But you do need muscles to carry one. Here, Schumer." He motioned for the moose to take his place.

"I'm honored!" Schumer said, bowing his head.

"We're doomed!" Boris wailed.

"I bet we look pretty funny walking around town like this," Crispin laughed. "You know, a few humans, a couple of animals and a giant map. We really stick out like a sore thumb."

Michael looked down at his thumbs and sighed with relief. *Good, mine are fine! Why would she say something like that?!?*

"It's not as uncommon as you might think," Orion said as they entered the forest. "Burlwood Forest Village was formed with both humans AND animals. Back then, we interacted all the time."

"Even without the necklaces?" Michael asked.

"Even without necklaces," Orion said, pointing to his own neck. He wasn't wearing one!

"But wait, how can you talk?" Crispin asked, confused. "Or at least, how COULD you talk?"

"There used to a be a little more magic back then," Orion shrugged. "Those of us from that time are just a little different, I guess. Plus, I'm the narrator, I HAVE to talk!"

"Getting really TIRED!" Boris yelled.

"Maybe we should tell him we don't need the map?" Michael laughed.

"Let him figure it out on his own," Stan said, walking up beside them. "I did."

"SOOOOO TIRED!!!!!" the bass player screamed.

"I'm doing fine!" Schumer reassured them, happily.

"He's going to screw something up, isn't he?" Stan asked, looking back at the moose.

"WHOA THAT DOESN'T FEEL GOOD LIKE AT ALL! WHOA! OUCH!" Boris yelled suddenly.

They stopped and looked behind them. Somehow, Schumer and Boris had ended up in a tree!

"I'm sorry! So, so sorry," the moose said apologetically. "I didn't mean to! This is my fault."

"Schumer, it's fine," Orion said, helping them down. "Why don't you leave the map up there and we can keep going? I think we can make it from here."

"Are you sure?" Schumer whimpered.

"Positive," the frog said, winking at Michael. They turned around and started to walk deeper into the forest.

WHAM!!!!

"What was THAT?!?" Michael asked, squeezing Crispin's hand tightly.

WHAM!!!!

"I don't know," Crispin said, too afraid to look around. She wasn't usually a big fan of scary noises.

WHAM!!!! WHAM!!! WHAM!!!

"It's interrupting the song in my head!" Michael said angrily. "Make it stop."

"Oh it won't stop," a sinister, but familiar, voice said. "But it WILL stop you."

Lieutenant Paul walked out from behind a tree, blocking the path in front of them. He was wearing the same strange necklace Michael had seen at the stadium.

Lord Piper's new weapon! Michael gasped.

Michael and Crispin turned around to warn the others, but it was too late. They had been knocked out!

"When he wakes up, I'll have to thank Schumer for slowing you guys down," Lieutenant Paul chuckled.

"Paul, you don't have to be this way," Michael pleaded his old friend.

"You're right, I don't," Paul smiled. "I chose this."

With the swift and familiar sound of a 'Wham!!!' Michael and Crispin were knocked out.

At least we'll get to the monastery, I guess...

Michael groaned and rolled over. He was laying on a hard surface that was definitely NOT in the forest. *Wayyyyy too many chapters of my life begin and end with me getting knocked out*, he thought.

He didn't want to open his eyes because he knew if he did, he would finally have to face Lord Piper. *I'm just not feeling that...*

But he didn't want to lay there forever either. It was cold! *Maybe I'll just keep my eyes closed and stand up anyway?* he thought. *I think that counts, but only sort of. That way, I won't have to fight anybody. At least, I hope not. Gosh, I hope not!*

Michael stood up and stretched his legs. He started to walk forward, hoping to find his friends so they could get out of there.

CRUNCH!

He stepped on something slightly hard, but slightly squishy. It kind of felt like a person.

"WHOA THAT DOESN'T FEEL GOOD LIKE AT ALL! WHOA! OUCH! OH WOW, WHOA!"

"Boris?" Michael asked. The bass player always yelled the same thing when he was hurt. *Thank goodness for that. I don't even have to open my eyes!*

"Dude, bro!" the bass player said. "GET OFF ME!"

Frowning, Michael stepped to the side. *It's not MY fault,* he thought. *I wasn't looking!*

BUMP!

"Sandwiches!" Michael yelled. He'd run into something else! It was tall, big and hairy.

"Grumpy Old Ms. Jones?!?!" he asked.

(Yuck.)

"Guess again, Michael. Guess again," Lieutenant Paul chuckled.

Crackers... "But you can't be Lieutenant Paul!" Michael said, confused. "Because if you were still here, then I would be like chained up or something. I thought maybe you had stepped away for a nice brunch, or mid-morning shower. Why am I free? What's up with that?"

"Lord Piper's orders," Paul chuckled. "He doesn't think you'll be stupid enough to try anything."

"Boy is HE wrong!" Michael said defiantly, backing up and tripping over something else. *This whole eyes closed thing is harder than I thought.*

"RIBBIT! RIBBIT!"

What the hey?!? Michael felt around until he found the source of the noise. It was a frog! *Awww gross!* he thought, flinging it to the other side of the room.

"Oh, there is ONE thing you should know," Lieutenant Paul said, kneeling down to face Michael. "Lord Piper rigged the monastery so only HIS animals can talk. I believe that was your friend, what do you call him? Orion? You just flung him against the wall. I'm sure he's fine though, really."

Ah, junk! Michael thought. Maybe keeping his eyes closed wasn't such a good idea after all! (Hindsight is so helpful, but REAL sight is, well...REALLY helpful too!)

"I'm going to open my eyes," Michael said.

"Please do, man!" Boris groaned.

"WHOA!" Michael yelled. He'd been missing out on a lot! They were in a large room with pretty awesome stained glass windows. "This looks like church!" he gasped.

"A monastery is where monks train," Lieutenant Paul said, amused. "And monks are people who devote their entire lives to God. It IS a church."

"Oh," Michael said, furrowing his brow. "I'd been wondering that the whole time."

"Please, let us go!" Grumpy Old Ms. Jones cried. She was huddled around the limp body of Orion with Boris, Crispin and Stan.

"Ha ha, let you go! You are funnier than I remembered!" Lieutenant Paul chuckled.

"I don't think we've actually met," Ms. Jones said. "There's a little bit of inconsistency here sometimes as to who actually knows who."

Horace and Griswald entered the room, pushing Schumer in front of them. He had a chain on his neck.

"He was looking for the bathroom!" the smaller of the two rats chuckled, pushing Schumer onto a large bench. "Don't worry though, we stopped him before he could get away!"

"You stopped him BEFORE he got to the bathroom?" Lieutenant Paul asked, angrily. "That was a terrible idea!"

"I told him," Griswald frowned. "He's a BAD rat."

"Oh, don't get me started on who's a 'bad rat,'" Horace snapped. "Didn't I catch you fluffing your pillows the other day?"

"What's wrong with that? I like to be comfortable!"

"But we're RATS! We're supposed to be filthy!"

"You're supposed to DO WHAT YOU'RE TOLD," Lieutenant Paul shouted. "Ah," he said, regaining his composure. "I forgot! Lord Piper wants to speak with you privately, Michael."

"Me?" Michael asked, confused. "Why me?"

"Because you're the main character of the story, dude!" Boris said, shrugging.

"Because we're too scared and we don't want to talk to him!" Stan whimpered.

Lieutenant Paul motioned for Michael to follow him. He pointed to the door of the confessional booth.

"Wait, why in there?" Michael asked. "He doesn't want to look into my eyes and see the fear and defeat? That's so unlike him."

"DON'T ask questions," the gorilla yelled, throwing the door open and shoving Michael inside. The lock turned with a 'click!'

Okay, okay, fine, Michael thought. He looked around, his eyes adjusting to the darkness. *This is curious. I wonder why Lord Piper is being so secretive? I mean, that IS his kind of thing, but more like secretive in a really open way. If that makes sense...*

"You may be wondering why I'm meeting you like this," Lord Piper said, his voice sending a chill up Michael's spine. "It is fitting that we're in a confessional, for I have a confession to make myself."

Why does he sounds so, like, sick? Michael thought, surprised. He began to wonder if there was something more than just secrecy behind the confessional booth.

"But I can tell you have something for me first, is that correct?" Lord Piper asked.

"You bet, I do," Michael said, nodding his head. "It's OVER! You've lost! You know, like, even though I'm being held captive right now."

The fox coughed, waiting patiently for Michael to continue.

This is so weird. I kind of want him to yell at me, Michael thought. He didn't really have anything else to say.

"Is that it?" Lord Piper asked, somewhat disappointed. "No details? No gloating?"

"Well, I mean, I'm not really that confident about it," Michael said, pausing. "I don't really know what you're doing with the whole necklace thing. And then there's Lieutenant Paul. He's alive, which is weird..."

(VERY weird.)

"Michael, Michael," the fox chuckled. "Don't sell yourself short! Just cause you ARE short doesn't mean you have to be! Go ahead, please. Seriously. Tell me how you've beaten me!"

"Good luck with that!" Michael said, angrily. "You don't even know what you're up against! Did you know there was a second group trying to bring you down?"

"You mean that stupid three legged cat and Dexterum Dei?" the fox said dismissively. "They've been taken care of."

"Yeah, by US!" Michael snapped.

"Whatever," Lord Piper chuckled. "It doesn't matter anyway! Right now, as we speak, Chet is putting new necklaces on your animal friends! When he's done, they'll all follow me! You'll ALL follow me! HAHAHAHAHA!"

(HAHAH...oh, wait. Sorry. Laughter is contagious.)

Michael didn't know how the fox could be so sure of himself. He had never been sure of anything!

"Why do you think I brought you into this box?" Lord Piper asked.

"Umm...because you like to play hide-and-seek?" Michael asked, hopefully.

"No, you fool! To get you out of the way! You may not be able to defeat me, but you've been a thorn in my side since day one! I'm not going to take it anymore! COUGH!"

"I don't think that's REALLY why you brought me here," Michael said quietly. He was beginning to put the pieces together. "You didn't bring me here because you didn't want to see ME. You brought me here because you didn't want me to see YOU!"

"What are you talking about? COUGH!" Lord Piper said. "Why in the world would I do that? COUGH! COUGH!"

"Because you're sick, aren't you?" Michael asked.

"Of COURSE NOT!" the fox said, angrily. "COUGH! This is all part of my plan! COUGH! COUGH! COUGH!"

"You LIAR!" Michael shouted. "I bet you tested the necklace on yourself and it backfired, didn't it? Didn't it? Hmmm? Hmmm?"

"More than you'll ever know," the fox said quietly. "It has done things to me I cannot take back. Things that have left me vulnerable. I've never felt this way before."

"So you're just going to hide?" Michael asked. "Is that your solution to everything?"

"Don't act like you're better than me!" the fox said. "You're no leader! You're an insecure, troubled little boy who's scared of the world. You've been ready to give up more times than you can count!"

Michael wanted to yell and tell Lord Piper he was wrong, but he wasn't. Even though he wanted to break out of the confessional and save his friends, he wanted nothing more than to be safe. Sometimes, that came at a price.

Just then, an explosion rocked the monastery. They had visitors.

The door of Michael's confessional booth burst open with a bang! Whatever had happened, had happened pretty quickly. He glanced around trying to figure out what was going on.

They're fighting back! he gasped. Michael smiled as members of the Nervous Sleeve ran past him. He shrugged and stepped back into the booth. *I'll join them in a second, but I want to watch this. It's like a movie! I LOVE movies!*

He reached into his pocket for some popcorn. *Drat! I forgot to put some in there,* he frowned. Fortunately, he was in luck. There was a bag of old carrots in the booth! *Strange, but oddly filling...*

While most of the Nervous Sleeve was engaged in the fight, Boris and Ms. Jones were getting, well...engaged!

"I was so worried if I didn't do this now it wouldn't happen," Boris said, pulling Ms. Jones aside and getting on one knee. "I wanted to do it at one of my band's shows, but I thought this would be just as good. I know it's not much, but I love you!" He handed Ms. Jones a small box, tears welling up in his eyes.

"You're supposed to open the box first!" Ms. Jones laughed, starting to cry too. She opened it up and smiled. Inside, there was a guitar pick that had been melted into the shape of a ring.

This movie has EVERYTHING! Action. Romance.

A pew flew across the room, smashing to pieces above Michael's head.

Danger...

The close encounter brought Michael back to his senses. His friends needed him! At least most of them. Probably not Boris and Ms. Jones. They were kissing. Michael couldn't think of anything he could do with that! They were doing a fine job themselves.

But who needed him the most? Stan and Orion were cornered by Lieutenant Paul. Schumer and Chet were nowhere to be seen. And Crispin...CRISPIN! She was fighting Horace and Griswald, right alongside the Club!

Wait...what club? Michael wondered.

Come on, Michael, you know, the Club! Go back and read Book 1. Remember the one with Sneaks, Boots, Snacks, Flip and Todd?

Right! I guess I just thought they'd play a bigger role in all this, Michael shrugged as he ran towards his friends.

(We all thought so, Michael. We all thought so...)

Surprised to see him coming, everyone stopped fighting. *Wow, I'm really good at this whole conflict resolution thing,* Michael thought. *Maybe I'll get my doctorate and become a relationship counselor?*

"Oh, look, Horace! Here he comes! I told you he'd come to save the girl, didn't I?" Griswald chuckled.

"YOU said that?" Horace said, shaking his head. "I said that! You said he'd sit in the confessional booth watching us fight like it was a movie!"

You're both right...

"Now, don't flatter yourself," Horace said, getting angry. "I was the one who said that and YOU know it!"

"Hey, why don't you BOTH shut it and let us go!" Sneaks snapped.

Well, that's what he WOULD have said if Lord Piper hadn't rigged the monastery so only his henchman could talk. It was unfortunate.

"I hate it when they make animal sounds like that, it's disgusting," Horace said, frowning. "It makes me feel like I need a shower."

"Now THAT'S something we can agree on!" Griswald said, clapping his paws together. "You DO need a shower!"

Horace knocked him to the ground.

"I knew you'd save us!" Crispin smiled brightly. "And I think I speak for all of us when I say that."

"I think you have to," Michael chuckled.

"HAHA!" Todd yelled, appearing out of the shadows and swooping down on top of their heads.

"Todd? Get off!" Michael yelled swatting at the eagle. "You're making my head itchy and you don't want to be around me when I'm itchy!"

"Probably not," Todd laughed. "But I have to pin you down while your friends die. LOOK!"

Michael turned and gasped. Chet had Stan backed into a corner and was trying to force one of Lord Piper's necklaces onto him. It wasn't working very well.

"Stop MOVING, Sherman! I can't get this over your big head!" the otter yelled angrily.

"Michael, WE HAVE TO DO SOMETHING!" Crispin screamed desperately.

Things weren't any better for Orion. Lieutenant Paul had him in a chokehold!

"RIBBIT! RIBBIT! RIBBIT! RIBBIT! RIBBIT! RIBBIT! RIBBIT! RIBBIT! RIBBIT!"

"Ah, there they go again. Those ANIMALS!" Horace gasped as Griswald dragged him back to the floor.

"Todd, please," Michael cried as he watched his friends struggle. "What happened to you?"

"I grew up!" Todd laughed. "Bald eagles are predators. Lord Piper showed me an article that said that online. It MUST be true! How could I resist?!?"

"Because Lord Piper is bad!" Michael said.

"You can do the right thing, Todd!" Crispin said."Haven't you read Sneaky Pete? Jefferson is a hero!"

"I don't have time for comic books," Todd scoffed, shaking his head. "I have more important things to do."

"No one. And I mean NO ONE. INSULTS SNEAKY PETE!" Michael growled.

Suddenly, he had an idea! Michael locked eyes with Crispin and she immediately knew what he wanted to do. *It's that thing where we only have one brain again*, he thought. Michael started to move to his left. Crispin started to move to her right.

"What are you doing?" Todd asked, his eyes wide. As they moved further away from him, the eagle's legs began to stretch too far! He readjusted his grip and dug his talons down further into their heads.

"Don't worry about it," Michael winced.

"Not sure I can do that," Todd said, puzzled. "It's starting to hurt quite a bit and that's kind of hard to ignore."

"Seriously," Michael mumbled. "NOW!" he yelled.

Michael and Crispin dove away from each other, sending Todd screeching around the room. Michael hit the floor hard, landing in front of the door. Two familiar faces smiled down at him.

It was Cephas and Mable! They'd finally made it to the monastery. He smiled back as Cephas helped him to his feet. Michael wasn't sure if his plan would work, but it was now or never. He looked behind them.

It was Chet's parents!

"Mom?!? Dad?!?" Chet asked, confused. "What the devil is going on? I told you not to disturb me at work!"

Chet's parents smiled and walked toward him.

"I'm warning you!" Chet said angrily. "Come any closer and the big guy gets it!" He grabbed Stan around the neck and squeezed tightly. The dog trainer's eyes looked like they were going to pop out, but thankfully, they didn't.

"This isn't having the effect I wanted it to," Michael said, leaning over to Crispin. "I was hoping Chet liked his parents enough to have a change of heart."

"Just wait," Crispin said, holding up her hand.

Engwald, Chet's father, walked over and put his arm around his son. Chet tried to shake him off.

"ERHHHH SDKJLD HERHHHHH ERHHHHH...." Engwald said, pointing at Chet's mother.

"I'm not sure what that means," Michael frowned, covering his ears. "What does that mean? Do you know what that means?"

"Shhh!!!" Crispin whispered, nudging him in the ribs. "Maybe it's in some sort of otter language?"

"Maybe," Michael said. "But why don't they offer that as an elective at school? That would help prepare me for the real world way better than MATH."

"SHHHHHHHH!!!!!!"

"I always knew you were foolish, but this takes the cake!" Chet smirked, pushing his father to the ground. "Did you think coming here would change anything? You always told me to follow my dreams! You always wanted me to be something. Well, look at me! For the first time in my life, I AM something. I AM somebody!"

Crying, Chet's father tried to stand up, but stumbled and fell back down. Chet's mother, Elmira, rushed to his side. "ERHHHHH SDKJLD HERHHHH ERHHHHHH!" Engwald yelled frantically, more insistent this time.

Michael could sense the frustration on the old otter's face. *What do I do?* he wondered. *What CAN I do?!?*

"I never wanted to be like you anyway," Chet shook his head. "Weak. Pathetic. I have everything I ever needed! Power. Fame. An endless supply of Mr. Sugar's Choco Squares! Don't you know we've already won? You're on the wrong side, Dad!"

"NOT SO FAST!" Schumer shouted triumphantly.

Michael whirled around and saw the moose standing across the room. He was holding a broken remote control in his hands.

"Where did you get that?" Chet asked angrily. "How are you talking? Stop it!"

"What is it?" Michael asked, furrowing his brow.

"I knew my absence would go unnoticed," Schumer said, throwing the remote to the ground. "So I set out to find whatever was keeping us from talking. I also still had to go to the bathroom so I did that too. But the remote wasn't hard to find. Especially since it's labeled 'SUPER EVIL DEVICE THAT KEEPS ANIMALS FROM TALKING.'"

"THAT'S WHAT YOU LABELED IT?" Lieutenant Paul growled. "I told you to DISGUISE IT!"

"THAT'S WHAT I DID, YOU WORTHLESS BABOON!" the otter yelled. "Haven't you ever heard of hiding something in plain sight?"

"Chet, your mother and I wanted to apologize," Engwald said, grabbing his wife's hand and squeezing it gently. "We never should have kicked you out of the house. We acted impulsively and didn't take the time to listen when you needed us the most. We're sorry for how much pain we've caused you. It's all we've been able to think about."

Chet looked like he was going to lash out again, but instead, released Stan and ran into his father's arms. "That's all I ever wanted to hear," he cried. "It's all I ever wanted. I love you, Dad."

"WHAT'S GOING ON?" Lord Piper yelled from the confessional booth. "ARE WE WINNING?!?"

"Chet's just turned all sappy, boss," Lieutenant Paul said, disgusted. "And Todd and those rats are worthless."

"WHAT?!?!?" Lord Piper asked, horrified. "That's it, I'm coming out."

"But sir, your condition..." Paul frowned.

"His what?" Crispin asked, confused.

The door of the confessional booth burst open. "I told you NOT to talk about that!" Lord Piper growled.

Michael gasped. The fox looked terrible. Even his signature sunglasses were cracked!

"Chet, what are you doing?" Lord Piper snapped.

The otter spit at Lord Piper's feet. "Doing what I should have done a long time ago, Patrick. I'm not bad! All I wanted was attention. And really, just attention from my parents. Now I have it. I don't need you."

"That's touching, really," Lord Piper scowled. "We'll be stronger without you then! You deserve what you'll get!" He leaned against the wall, looking weak.

"NOT SO FAST!" Tugley yelled. As he entered the room, he was followed closely by Moe, Ralph, Miss Dandelion and Grandpa Pumpernickel.

There are wayyyy too many people in this room, Michael thought, trying to count them on his hands before giving up. *I hope a fire marshal doesn't read this book.*

"What do you mean, not so fast!" Lord Piper said.

"Well, that's what I heard this fellow over here say," Tugley said, gesturing at Schumer.

"What are you doing with them? They're the BAD GUYS!" Lord Piper yelled.

"I'm working with them," Tugley said, smiling. "And I have been for a long time."

"The double agent!" Michael gasped before he could stop himself. "Oh," he said quickly. "I'm sorry. I didn't mean to reveal your secret."

"It's quite alright, Michael," Tugley chuckled. "I was about to do that myself."

"What's going on?" Lord Piper snapped, looking around the room. "Am I missing something?"

"Give it to him," Ralph said, turning to his grandfather. "It's time."

The old man nodded and pulled something out of his fanny pack. It was a blue and white striped shirt with a green collar.

"What's the meaning of this?" Lord Piper asked, backing up. "Why do you have that?"

"I believe you recognize it, don't you, Piper?" Orion asked, stepping forward. "It was yours once. When you were a boy here."

"It might have been, but I AM NO LONGER THAT BOY!" the fox said angrily. "Paul, seize them!"

Lieutenant Paul charged. Grandpa Pumpernickel knocked him to the ground and smashed the mind control necklace with his fist. "Men shouldn't wear jewelry!" he growled.

Whoa. The things you learn in prison!

"Wait...where am I?" Paul asked, looking dazed.

"Piper," Grandpa Pumpernickel said.

"LORD PIPER!" the fox screamed.

"No," Orion said, shaking his head. "Just Piper. Remember," he said, tossing him the shirt. It landed at the fox's feet.

"When I first met you, you were so young, so full of energy," Orion laughed. "The other monks thought that you were trouble, but I knew better. You were just a boy! I always knew of course, that the monastic lifestyle was not for you. That's okay, it wasn't for me either. At least the one promoted by the abbot."

"The evil three-legged cat?" Michael asked.

"Yes, Michael," Orion said, nodding. "The very one that nearly took your brother's life. You see, once he was appointed, it didn't take long for many of us to realize his true intentions. He cared more for power than he ever did for God!"

"That's terrible!" Crispin said. "Why didn't you do anything?"

"I tried, but many of my fellow monks were too scared!" Orion sighed. "They thought they should follow the authority God placed over them. I don't think God had anything to do with it!"

"What's your point?" Lord Piper snapped, avoiding eye contact.

"Piper, I don't want to fight you," Orion said. "We've both been hurt by the abbot, but that doesn't mean we don't want the same thing. Let go of your anger. What's in the past is in the past. Pain is strong, but love is stronger! I know all of us in this room have done things we regret.

We can only move forward with the understanding that we're not perfect. No one is."

Lord Piper didn't say anything. He was staring at the shirt.

"I remember when I first met you too," Grandpa Pumpernickel chuckled. "Boy, was I surprised! Animals that could talk! But once the shock wore off, I realized you were MORE than a novelty. You were a friend. I know you may never forgive me for siding with the others, but it was the hardest decision I've ever made. I never meant to hurt you."

Grandpa Pumpernickel nudged Michael in the ribs.

Ouch! Michael thought. *Oh! I guess we're all taking turns here.* He took a deep breath. "Lord Piper, when I first got your letter, I was really excited."

"What?" Crispin asked. "Are you crazy?"

"Wait," Michael said, holding his hand up. "I'm getting to the good part. I had never gotten any mail before so it wouldn't have mattered what the letter said. Really. It just felt good to be included! I've gone through a lot these past few years, and I'm not even eleven anymore. I've been angry. I've been confused. I've been upset. I've even been tied to the underside of my desk."

"We didn't do that," Todd said, frowning.

"I know," Michael chuckled. "That's what I get for not doing my math homework."

"What?" Ms. Jones asked.

"Anyway," Michael said. "What I'm trying to say is that I understand where you're coming from. We ARE the same. Every time we've talked you tried to tell me that. I think I finally understand what you meant. You're not a bad person, Piper, and I'm not either. Everyone needs someone to believe in them. Let us be that for you."

Michael looked from Crispin, to his brother, to Mable. Orion was right. None of them were perfect. But they needed someone. They needed each other.

Suddenly, Lord Piper started to cry.

"Lord Piper, what's wrong?" Ralph asked.

"It's just Piper, thanks," Lord Piper (sorry, PIPER) said. "For so long I hardened my heart. To anyone, anything that reminded me of this place. To family. To

God. I chose the name 'Lord Piper' in defiance of what the abbot stood for. But now, I realize he didn't represent God at all. All my life, I've wondered where I came from. I lashed out at everyone because I wanted a family. I never realized I was pushing the one I had away," he said, smiling at them. "I'm sorry to all of you. I really am. I hope you can forgive me."

"Of course we can!" Michael smiled. "But now what? The forest is almost gone. You cut it down..."

"I think I can help you there," Piper said, walking over to a small, wooden box. "I saved these, you know, just in case." He tipped over the box and thousands of seeds poured out onto the ground!

(Great. Now someone has to clean that up.)

"I always believed in you, Piper," Orion said. "And now, I think you believe in yourself."

All of a sudden, a bear came bursting into the room.

"RAWRRRRR RAWRRRRRR RAWRRRRR!" the bear said before frowning and tapping his throat. "I'm sorry," he said. "I didn't realize I could talk normally now. I've been hibernating, what did I miss?"

"Phineas?" Cephas asked, confused.

"Oh, hey, Cephas," the bear chuckled. "How's life, man? You haven't seen my cousin, Ruxiben, around, have you? His mom told me he was supposed to hibernate with the pack this year, but I haven't seen him in six months."

"Ruxiben is your COUSIN?!?!?" Michael asked.

"Well, sure," Phineas shrugged. "He's not out selling again, is he? Ruxiben gets kind of carried away."

"Oh my goodness, oh my goodness!" Grohill said, rushing into the room. He shrieked when he saw everyone, diving behind a pew. "Lord Piper, sir!" his said, his voice muffled. "There's a bear loose in the monastery!"

"I know, Grohill, I know," Piper chuckled.

"GROHILL?!?!?!" Michael asked.

The porcupine shrieked again, covering his head.

"It's okay, Grohill," Piper said. "We're friends now."

"What?!?" Grohill squealed. "We are? But...I betrayed everyone in this room! Isn't that bad?"

"We forgive you," Lieutenant Paul smiled.

318

"You do?" the porcupine asked, slowly coming out from behind the bench.

"We do," Michael said. He grinned at his old friend, glad they could finally be honest with each other.

"Well, now that that's settled, it's time for me to go," Piper said abruptly, wincing as he walked toward the door.

"What?!? Where are you going?" Grandpa Pumpernickel asked, confused.

"To find my family of course! My REAL family! Even though you guys aren't half bad," the fox chuckled. "I've wasted far too much time! You're coming with me, aren't you?"

"I am?" Grandpa Pumpernickel asked, surprised. "It...it would be an honor."

"We have to go too," Mable said, walking towards the pile of seeds. "We have a forest to replant!"

"Wait!" Michael said. "Aren't we all going to hug? I need closure!"

In no time, he was alone in the monastery with Crispin. *Oooooooo nevermind,* he thought. *I like this!*

"We need to go too, Michael," Crispin said, putting a hand on his back.

"It all happened so fast," Michael said, frowning. *Adventures are supposed to conclude!!!*

"I know," Crispin said, smiling. "But if we don't hurry, we'll be late. We have somewhere to be too."

"But where?" Michael asked, confused. "We defeated Lord Piper. Or rather, didn't, because we didn't have to. It's all over!"

"One thing isn't over yet," she said, laughing. "School!"

Michael grinned. He took her hand and they ran out the door together.

"Michael Pumpernickel?"

"HOLY CROW! Ms. Jones actually said my name during roll call!" Michael yelled.

"Michael, don't talk out of turn!" the teacher scolded.

"But you just said my name. Aren't I supposed to talk? White rabbits! She acknowledged me in public!" Michael said excitedly, turning to Crispin.

Ms. Jones smiled, shaking her head. "I guess you're right. But I'm not Ms. Jones anymore, you should know that. I'm Mrs. Frankfurter! Didn't you pay attention at my wedding?"

(The reception was wonderful!)

"You were at her WEDDING? That's SOOOOOOO WEIRDDDDDDDDD," Jasper laughed, slapping his desk.

When he realized no one else was laughing with him, he stopped and frowned, crossing his arms.

"We're SO happy to have you back, Mr. Clemmons!" Mrs. Frankfurter said.

"I'm not," Michael shrugged.

"I'm not either," Tommy Snaggletooth grumbled. He couldn't be the bully anymore.

"And how do YOU feel about it, Jasper," Mrs. Frankfurter asked.

The bully paused, deep in thought. "I guess this place is okay. I mean, I didn't really like being off at boarding school. Plus, I'm really excited to be in the same class as Michael again so I can MAKE HIM PAY FOR WHAT HE DID TO MY DAD!!!!!"

The class stared at him and started talking amongst themselves. Jasper sighed.

"I'm glad to see some things don't change," Michael laughed, leaning back in his seat.

"Well that's not exactly true," Crispin smiled. "You're back in school."

"I never really left. I was here in spirit," Michael said, winking.

"Okay, then. What about my dad? Hungry Woody's is back!"

"I know. I'm not sure my stomach can handle that," Michael grimaced.

"Oh, stop!" Crispin laughed, playfully punching him on the shoulder. "How about YOUR family then? Your father and your Grandpa are on good terms. He even lives with you!"

"My dad always lived with me."

"Not your dad, your GRANDPA!" Crispin laughed.

"Oh yeah..."

"And what about your brother and Boris?"

"What about them?" Michael asked, confused.

"They started a BAND! Boris is ACTUALLY in a band now! Not to mention they run a music venue/restaurant on the side."

"I guess that's something," Michael shrugged.

- THE END -

"Michael Pumpernickel, you're impossible," Crispin chuckled. "Everything worked out, didn't it? The good guys won. The bad guys became good. Everything is how it should be."

"Is it, Miss Rye?" Mrs. Frankfurter asked, folding her arms. "Are you and Mr. Pumpernickel done with the very personal epilogue of the past two years of your life?"

"Maybe," Michael said. "But I could go on forever."

"We know you can, Michael," Mrs. Frankfurter said, smiling. "But it will have to wait. Seriously, WAIT."

"But I hadn't gotten to the part where I was going to tell Crispin that I'm a crime fighter now!" Michael frowned. "She was going to be impressed and go out with me!"

"She already goes out with you," Mrs. Frankfurter sighed.

"Good point. Should I still tell her?" Michael asked, scratching his head.

"If you would like," Mrs. Frankfurter sighed.

Just then, someone knocked on the door. It was Michael's old math tutor, Lucy Peterson.

What is SHE doing here?!?!? Michael wondered. *I'm SO over that.*

"I'm sorry to interrupt, Mrs. Frankfurter," Lucy said apologetically. "But this accidentally got delivered to the high school. I think it's for one of your students, isn't it?"

Mrs. Frankfurter looked at the envelope in Lucy's hand and nodded. "Thank you, Lucy."

Lucy smiled and closed the door. Before she did, Michael could have sworn she looked at him and growled.

Whatever...

"Crispin?" Mrs. Frankfurter said. "It's for you."

Crispin looked at Michael and slowly walked to the front of the room. She took the envelope out of Mrs. Frankfurter's hands and returned to her seat, a curious expression on her face.

"Who is it from?" Michael whispered (far too loudly as he always does). "Is it a love letter from me? I can't remember if I wrote one."

"It's from someone with the initials 'BVQ,'" Crispin said. "Who's 'BVQ'?"

- THE END -

"Is that a type of sandwich?" Michael asked hopefully. "Because if it's a sandwich, I'll split it with you. I've only had lunch once today."

"No," Crispin said, tearing open the envelope. "It must be a person. Look."

Disappointed, Michael leaned over to read the mysterious letter-

Crispin,

I hope this letter finds you well. I fear that it could fall into the wrong hands, so please, show this to NO ONE!"

Crispin clutched the letter close to her chest, blocking it from Michael's view. Michael frowned and crossed his arms. Crispin sighed, putting it back down.

"I am writing from a secure location. I don't think they suspect I'm the one looking for it, but if they do, we could all be in danger. Something big is about to happen, and I'm sure that you are the only one who can help me. Please, Crispin. If the fate of our world means anything to you, meet me at..."

"Meet me at where?!?" Michael asked, grabbing the letter. "Meet me at where?!?"

"I don't know," Crispin said. "It's all smudged at the end." She snatched the letter back and squinted at the bottom.

"Do you think he's left-handed?" Michael gasped.

"What does that have to do with anything?" Crispin wondered. "Do you think he got captured?"

"I don't know," Michael frowned. "If he got captured, would he still be able to seal the letter and go to the post office to mail it?"

"Probably not, but what if he wasn't the one who did?" Crispin said, worriedly. "What if someone else mailed it?"

"Isn't that a felony?" Michael asked, scratching his head.

"No. Not at all."

Crispin and Michael stared at the letter, not saying a word. As Mrs. Frankfurter began the lesson for the day, all they could think about was the mysterious 'BVQ.' Who was he? What was he up to? And why would he send a letter to Crispin when Michael had just started his own crime fighting business under the terrifying name, 'The Pink Polo?'

We may never know. Or, we MAY know someday. We'll see. But as Michael sat there, ignoring school for the first time EVER, on his first day back no less, he couldn't help but think one thing.

I'm hungry....

John Choquette is the author of Burlwood Forest, and the owner of Pumpernickel Art, a lifestyle design and publishing company founded in 2015. He received a B.A. in journalism from The University of North Carolina at Chapel Hill, and lives in the Triangle area with his amazing wife.

Visit him online at www.burlwoodforest.com to stay up-to-date on the amazing things he's up to.

Made in the USA
Charleston, SC
08 January 2017